“Have a seat.”

Charlie’s tone was hard as she pointed to the empty chair next to her.

As Detective Grayson Leigh sat down, she handed him a thick notebook. “This is the Goins murder book. I assume you’ve read up on the case?”

He nodded. “Yes, ma’am.”

“Good. We don’t have time for any slacking off,” Charlie said, her voice curt. “Since we’re being forced to work together on this, I won’t tolerate any incompetence. Understand?”

Grayson clenched his jaw and looked straight ahead. He could feel Charlie’s eyes on him, but he needed to whisper a prayer for patience. He had been with the Cold Case Unit for five years. He knew how to do his job.

“Here’s the first responder’s report as well as my notes. Melanie’s death was a violent one. The weapon, a knife, wasn’t found. It’s still missing.” She stopped for a second, then asked, “Are you listening to me?”

“Yeah,” he replied, glancing down at the second page of the report. “I’m still wading through the detailed notes from your initial audit and something in particular caught my eye...”

Jacquelin Thomas is an award-winning, bestselling author with more than fifty-five books in print. When not writing, she is busy catching up on her reading, attending sporting events and spoiling her grandchildren. Jacquelin and her family live in North Carolina.

Books by Jacquelin Thomas

Love Inspired Suspense

Sorority Cold Case

Love Inspired Cold Case

Evidence Uncovered
Cold Case Deceit

Love Inspired The Protectors

Vigilante Justice

Harlequin Heartwarming

A Family for the Firefighter
Her Hometown Hero
Her Marine Hero
His Partnership Proposal
Twins for the Holidays

Visit the Author Profile page at LoveInspired.com.

Sorority Cold Case

JACQUELIN THOMAS

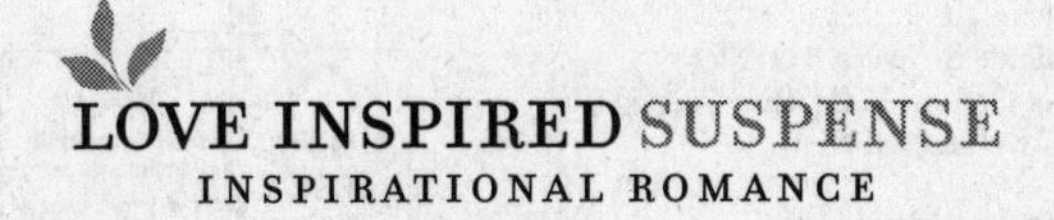

Recycling programs for this product may not exist in your area.

ISBN-13: 978-1-335-98012-0

Sorority Cold Case

For questions and comments about the quality of this book, please contact us at CustomerService@Harlequin.com.

Love Inspired
22 Adelaide St. West, 41st Floor
Toronto, Ontario M5H 4E3, Canada
www.LoveInspired.com

Printed in Lithuania

Therefore if any man be in Christ,
he is a new creature: old things are passed away;
behold, all things are become new.
—*2 Corinthians* 5:17

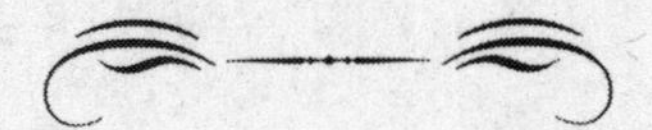

ONE

Every detective has at least one case they can never forget. Charlotte Tesarkee, who preferred to be called Charlie, had been haunted by the death of Melanie Goins for eleven years. She had been obsessed with the case ever since she was the lead investigator and had failed to find the person responsible. Her gut told her that she had possibly been close to solving it, but back then Charlie couldn't quite put all the pieces together. After eighteen months, she was pulled off the investigation, leaving the case to go cold. However, she refused to give up on finding the college student's killer. Melanie was the main reason behind Charlie's request to transfer into the Cold Case Unit—CCU—at the Charlotte-Mecklenburg Police Department. She'd been there for two months now.

She sat at her desk in the CCU, scrolling through the case file on her computer screen, her eyes scanning over the same details she's read countless times before. Nineteen-year-old Melanie Goins was found dead in her dorm room. She had been stabbed twenty-two times. Near her body was a pillow with a single blue feather—a symbol of the sorority's Indigenous heritage—embroidered on it, a wine bottle and a note.

Charlie's throat tightened as she thought of Melanie's family, their grief and confusion without any closure. Taking a steadying breath, she determinedly returned her attention to the case file, hoping to uncover enough evidence to bring the criminals to justice.

After a few hours of examining all the little details, Charlie stood up, ready to walk to her supervisor's office with a plan—she was going to propose the idea of using new technology available to trace DNA ancestry in order to find the culprit responsible for Melanie's death.

She glanced up at the framed painting hanging near her desk: a deer lying in a grassy field, full of colors woven together in harmony. For a moment, Charlie imagined herself in the forest with the animal, allowing the peacefulness and melodious sound of nature to wash over her before standing up and walking across the hall.

Her mind made up, she knocked on Captain Phillipa Stevenson's door.

"Come in."

Charlie stepped inside the midsize office, decorated with four tall bookcases in a rich walnut color against a gray wall. To her right, bright sunlight filtered through the open pale gray blinds which offered teasing views of the uptown Charlotte skyline. Her feet felt the office carpet beneath her, thick and plush, softer than the outside sidewalk with its broken concrete and dirt.

Phillipa sat behind a wooden desk in walnut with an ornate border near the edge. "Good morning, Charlie. What can I do for you?"

She sat down in one of the chairs facing her supervisor. "There's a case I worked when I was in Homicide. I worked that investigation until every single lead grew cold," Charlie responded. "In a couple months, the case will be eleven years old. I'd like to revisit it."

"Summarize the case for me?"

"On September sixth, eleven years ago, the victim and her roommate left their off-campus apartment, heading out to a club. The roommate felt unwell, so she and the victim left the club around two in the morning. The victim went to bed while her roommate left to stay with a friend for the remainder of the night. The roommate returned home the next morning, found the victim's door open and her body. Evidence found was a note saying, 'I'm not stupid.' There was also a wine bottle lying on the floor and a small square pillow stained with the victim's blood. We know that the victim drank a couple glasses the night she died. The wineglass was on the nightstand. We were able to pull a print off the bottle."

"Was there a second glass anywhere in the room or was she drinking alone?" Phillipa asked.

"The crime scene pointed to her drinking alone."

"Do you have any new evidence?"

Charlie shook her head no. "With all the technology we have available to us now—I'd like to submit the prints we found in the apartment for DNA ancestry testing. As you know, DNA fingerprinting doesn't always turn up viable leads."

Nodding, Phillipa said, "So you'd like to see if forensic genealogy will generate investigative leads in this specific case. What other evidence do you have?"

"DNA evidence was collected from under the victim's fingernails."

"Which case is it?"

"Melanie Goins."

"I'll review the file, then make a decision by end of day," Phillipa said.

"Fair enough," Charlie responded as she rose to her feet.

"After today, I'll be out of the office for ten days," Phillipa announced. "The wedding is this weekend and I still have so much left to do. Kyle and I didn't want anything huge, but there's still a lot which goes into the planning."

"I can imagine," Charlie replied, but deep down she didn't understand at all, being more of a *justice of the peace* kind of girl. She never dreamed of fancy wedding gowns, beautiful and exotic flowers—all the stuff that little girls often dreamed of... Truth be told, Charlie never even fantasized about a husband because she didn't believe marriage was in her future.

She felt compelled to attend the ceremony and reception because Phillipa and Kyle, who was the unit supervisor of Robbery, had invited both their teams to the wedding. However, Charlie wasn't thrilled with the idea of getting dressed up, nor was she looking forward to spending off-duty hours with her coworkers. Though Charlie wanted to keep her relationships on a professional level, deep down she yearned for true connection, but nothing could fill the void of her parents' lack of love and security.

Growing up, Charlie worked hard, trying to make them just notice her; she wanted to make them proud, but then she ended up in foster care. Her heart ached with loneliness, but she was determined to never let anyone get close to her. Life experiences had taught her that trust was hard to come by, and yet she still hoped for someone to prove her wrong.

Grayson Leigh stood outside the police precinct, taking in the calm surroundings. He hesitated for a moment before stepping inside, his mind racing with possibilities. The scent of fresh air filled his nostrils and gave him a sense of clarity.

Six months ago, on his forty-fifth birthday, Grayson left the station and narrowly survived a terrible car accident. The drunk driver who hit him didn't survive. Before that life-changing moment in time he was arrogant. He'd always thought very highly of himself, even considered himself invincible. Some called him a narcissist. But it didn't matter how others saw him because Grayson didn't care.

The horrific accident left Grayson in unimaginable agony: a broken arm and leg, painfully throbbing internal injuries. He was overcome with despair, and there were days when he felt death would be the sweetest relief from his suffering. Yet Grayson refused to give up; he was determined to live. The experience changed him profoundly, reminding him of his vulnerability and mortality as a human being.

After months of healing and rigorous physical therapy, he had become a different man. The pain was unbearable, but Grayson dug deep within himself to muster the strength to keep going. This experience served as an opportunity for him to learn how strong a man he could truly be. Although Grayson remained unbothered by others' opinions of him, his perspective on life in general had changed. He knew without a doubt that it was God who saved him. The near-fatal accident made him evaluate his life and wonder about God's purpose.

Grayson stood there, silently willing his body to enter the building. Physically, he was ready to get back to work. He even felt mentally prepared, but Phillipa hadn't seemed completely convinced when they discussed his return last week.

The doors opened and Jason Langford, a detective, walked outside.

"Detective Leigh, I was beginning to wonder if you were ever coming back," he said. "Man…it's great to see you."

"I'm happy to be seen and not viewed," Grayson responded.

Jason grinned. "I have to go serve this warrant and pick up this dude, but when I get back—we have to talk. I can't wait to catch up with you."

"Sounds good," he said before walking inside.

Grayson paused a moment as his eyes adjusted to the fluorescent lights illuminating the dull beige walls and floors which carried a year's worth of blemishes and age worn into them.

He saw cops leaving after roll call and a journalist attempting to cover a story. A couple officers leaned against the front desk, laughing with the receptionist. The clock on the wall ticked the seconds away loudly; each tick was like a century, each bell a millennium.

He took the elevator up to the CCU department.

Grayson locked gazes with Detective Charlie Tesarkee almost immediately. She eyed him with obvious contempt before looking away.

For as long as he'd known her, Charlie kept her silky hair cut short in a pixie style, the black color gleaming like a raven's plumage. Her high cheekbones looked like a fine chisel had been passed over them to create the shape of her face. The edges of her eyes and nose turned up, the nostrils slightly flared. Her clear, smooth skin was the color of golden honey, her brown eyes matching the color of his own. Only there wasn't an ounce of warmth in her gaze. She stood almost six feet tall with an athletic build.

When did she transfer to CCU? he wondered. Grayson had worked with her in the Homicide department before he left to join the cold case unit five years ago. During that time, Charlie was abrasive and very defensive. It wasn't completely directed at him—she was like that with everyone. Although the detectives in the department tried to be inclusive, Charlie refused to allow anyone to get close to her. He was only too happy to leave her behind. Now she was here in CCU and sitting at his old desk.

It doesn't matter where you sit, he told himself. *Just smile and keep it moving.*

"Good morning," Grayson said, pausing briefly at her desk.

"What are you doing here?" Charlie blurted.

"I'm healthy, so I figured it's time for me to get back to work."

"Oh." She returned her attention to her computer.

Biting back a smile, Grayson continued walking briskly toward Phillipa's office.

"Grayson, it's so good to see you," she stated warmly, rising to her feet when he appeared in the doorway.

"I'm ready to get back to work," he said without preamble. "*I need this.* I'm not a huge television person or much of a homebody. I need more in my life."

"I see that your doctor cleared you," Phillipa responded.

"But you still have some concerns," Grayson interjected. "There's nothing to worry about. I'm *good.* No PTSD from the accident. I sleep fine at night..."

"I just have to be sure. You suffered a terrible accident. From what I understand it was touch and go for a while there. I just want to make sure you're not rushing things. Grayson, I told you that your job would be here waiting on you. I meant what I said."

He smiled. "I understand. Just know that you have nothing to worry about. I'm a hundred percent. I'm willing to take a psych eval if necessary."

"I have to make sure," Phillipa said hastily, followed by a softer, "I'm glad you're back, Grayson. There's a case here I think you'll be perfect for." She picked up the receiver and dialed. "Charlie needs to get in here. You two will be working on the Goins case together."

Grayson felt a jolt of electricity shoot through his veins at the mention of Charlie. "Goins? Isn't that the college student who was killed near the university?" he asked.

"You're familiar with the case?"

He nodded. "I also remember that Charlie was the lead detective on that investigation."

Phillipa leaned forward in her chair, her eyes fixed on Grayson's face. "She requested that we reopen the case," she stated, her voice low and intense. "I spoke to Commander Peters a few minutes ago about it—I had to convince him that this wouldn't be a waste of time and taxpayer dollars. Charlie's a great detective but I'd like for you to work with her. I think the two of you working together could close the case."

Grayson paused before responding. He knew instinctively that Charlie would go ballistic when she found out. "Does she know this?"

Phillipa shook her head. "Not yet," she responded. "She's about to find out."

He didn't know anyone who *willingly* wanted to partner with her—Charlie didn't play well with others. The truth was that he wasn't exactly thrilled with the idea either, but was motivated to prove that he was physically and mentally fit to return to the job. Despite his personal feelings about Charlie, Grayson was going to find a way to get along with her. The Goins investigation depended on them working together.

Charlie stepped into Phillipa's office, barely acknowledging Grayson with a brief glance as she tried to suppress the dislike she felt for him. She couldn't imagine why Phillipa requested that she join them.

But as soon as her supervisor began speaking, Charlie dreaded what was sure to come out of her mouth. "I read through the Goins case and I think you should take a shot at finding justice for this victim. Commander Peters had some reservations but I convinced him that this case deserved another look."

"Thank you," Charlie responded, relieved that she had another chance to find Melanie's killer.

"There's only one stipulation, however..." Phillipa said. "Charlie, I want Grayson to partner with you."

"I don't need a partner for this," she blurted. "I worked this case originally. He doesn't know a thing about it."

But Phillipa was adamant. "Grayson will bring fresh eyes and perspective to the investigation," she said firmly.

Charlie reluctantly acquiesced, though her heart felt heavy with dread. On the outside, she seemed strong and unyielding, but on the inside, emotions from her turbulent childhood threatened to overwhelm her. The last person she wanted to work alongside was Grayson. She truly couldn't stand the man, especially after the way he'd betrayed her when he was supposed to be mentoring her at the time. She'd looked to him for guidance for her first homicide investigation. The next day, the case was reassigned to Grayson.

Her already thorny exterior was the result of a childhood littered with parental emotional abandonment and alcoholism. Growing up, she had been extremely shy and timid, so she retreated into a fantasy world born out of the many books she read. Once Charlie found her voice, she vowed to never allow anyone to ever silence her again. She had confronted her supervisor and Grayson, and ended up with a suspension and a stern warning.

Charlie knew that her outspoken nature made people think she was aggressive and impulsive, but she couldn't help it. Standing up for the oppressed and bringing justice to those who had been silenced was deeply important to her, especially when it came to Melanie Goins. Charlie identified with the victim—they were both Indigenous, black and members of the Native American Alpha Pi Omega sorority—so finding the murderer became a personal mission for her.

"If that's all, I'd like to get started on my investigation," Charlie stated before leaving the office. She didn't want a repeat of what happened in Homicide, so she kept her frustration to herself.

She sat down at her desk, taking several cleansing breaths.

How could Phillipa do this to me? Charlie felt as if she'd been stabbed in the back, betrayed yet again.

When Grayson walked out of their supervisor's office minutes later, he didn't glance in her direction this time. Glaring at his back, Charlie bristled with white-hot anger.

This was not going to work for her, but there was nothing she could do about it. Complaining to Phillipa might get her taken off the case and Charlie didn't want to sit on the sidelines while someone else worked the investigation. Eleven years ago, she'd promised Melanie's mother and uncle that she'd never give up on finding the killer and she intended to keep her word. Besides, Charlie refused to give Grayson the satisfaction of running her off.

Taking another deep breath, she turned away from him. She couldn't afford to let her emotions get the best of her, not when the investigation was at a critical stage. Melanie's killer was still out there, and they needed to catch the person responsible this time.

When she was calm, Charlie headed to the break room for coffee. She would find a way to make this work with Grayson, however, she was the lead detective—it was *her* case.

Her coworker Jen was the only person in there. She was of average height with buttery smooth dark skin and friendly brown eyes, her shoulder-length hair pulled into a low bun. She finished up her pastry, then flicked something off her uniform. "Charlie, I was just thinking about you. We need to plan something nice for your birthday next month."

"Jen…you know I don't want anything big. I'm happy with just lunch and a card." She poured hot coffee into the mug she'd brought with her. Turning forty just wasn't a big deal for Charlie. Maybe it was because her parents never did anything to celebrate any of her birthdays—to them, it was just another day and a reminder that she was nothing more than an inconvenience. Her foster parents attempted to throw parties for her, but Charlie refused to participate so they eventually gave up.

"That won't do," Jen uttered. "We celebrate birthdays…you know that. I don't know why I have to go through this with you every year."

Charlie took a sip. "I keep hoping you'll give up on this idea."

Jen shook her head. "Not gonna happen."

"See you later."

As Charlie approached her workstation, she felt a complicated mix of emotions. On the one hand, she was filled with determination to solve the case and bring Melanie's killer to justice. But on the other hand, she dreaded the thought of working with Grayson again. Once more, he was standing in the way of her success. But she was not about to back down from her mission. If that meant having to work alongside Grayson, then so be it; she would do whatever it took to achieve justice.

TWO

Grayson knew he needed to find a way to approach Charlie that would make her want to work with him instead of against him. He picked up the receiver and dialed her extension, feeling a sense of trepidation as he waited for her to pick up.

"Hello?" Charlie's voice was gruff, as usual.

"Hey, it's Grayson."

Silence.

"Listen, I really want to make this partnership work. I know how important the Goins case is to you. I know we can solve it if we work together."

There was a long pause on the other end of the line, and Grayson held his breath, waiting for Charlie's response.

"Fine," she finally said. "But I'm telling you now…you better not try to undermine me like you did before. Stay out of my way."

Grayson let out a sigh of relief. It was far from a warm welcome, but it was a start.

"We can work in one of the empty conference rooms," Charlie was saying. "I'll book one from eleven to one o'clock."

He strode into the conference room at ten-fifty to find Charlie already there, seated at the head of the table. Her steely gaze met his as he entered, and Grayson could tell she was trying to intimidate him. He took a deep breath and prepared himself for what was about to come.

"Have a seat," Charlie said curtly, pointing to the empty chair next to her.

As Grayson sat down, she handed him a thick notebook. "This is the Goins murder book. You can read up on the case."

He nodded. "Yes, ma'am. Just so you know, I followed your case when it happened."

"Good. We don't have time for any slacking off," Charlie said. "Since we're being forced to work together on this, I want you to know I don't trust you and I'll be watching every move you make. Understand?"

Grayson clenched his jaw and looked straight ahead. He could feel Charlie's eyes on him, but he refused to make eye contact. He needed to whisper a prayer for patience—something he didn't have in this moment. He had been with the CCU for five years. He knew how to do his job. Grayson knew Charlie was still upset with him because of a case that was taken from her and reassigned to him during their homicide days. She was new to the unit and it was her first investigation. Their supervisor back then had treated her unfairly, but Charlie turned her wrath toward him. Grayson never forgot the seething look she'd given him when he closed the case. It was a look of complete betrayal.

"Here's the first responder's report as well as my notes." She handed the document to him. "Melanie's death was a violent one—she was stabbed to death twenty-two times in the abdomen, lower torso, neck and chin. She also sustained some facial injuries. She didn't go down without a fight, however. CSI found evidence from beneath her nails. The weapon, a knife, wasn't found in her home… unfortunately, it's still missing. The only other evidence in her bedroom was an empty wine bottle lying near her body, a bloodstained pillow, and a note with 'I'm not stupid' written across it. Back then I thought that maybe it was the killer who wrote it…" Charlie stopped for a second, then asked, "Are you listening to me?"

"Yeah," he replied after glancing down at the second page of the report. "No evidence found to indicate sexual assault. I'm still wading through the detailed notes from your initial audit and something in particular caught my eye."

Leaning forward, she asked, "What?"

"The victim and her roommate left the club due to the roommate feeling sick, then shortly after they arrived back home, that same roommate departed again." He took a deep breath. "The fact that she left the door unlocked… But let's put that aside for now. I'd prefer to just wait until I read the witness and suspect statements."

"Okay. Sure," she responded.

Grayson bit back a smile when he caught a glimmer of surprise in her gaze. He returned his attention to the notes. "Tell me about the day you saw the victim and the crime scene."

"The sight of Melanie's body left me shaking," Charlie said. "She was ravaged by a ruthless attack. There was so much blood…so much unnecessary violence inflicted upon her. I felt an immediate connection to her—not only did we share the same sorority and Indigenous identity but also, I felt responsible for justice, as if it was my duty to speak for her and make sure no one ever forgot this atrocity."

Grayson nodded in understanding.

"I can't fail her a second time," she stated. "Every year since Melanie's death, I've gone over my notes, interviews… everything. I keep trying to figure out what I missed."

"You shouldn't automatically assume that you've missed something. There are still clues to be revealed."

"I know," Charlie responded. "I plan on revisiting every inch of this investigation. Starting with the 9-1-1 call made by the victim's roommate, Kathy Dixon."

Grayson listened to the recording a couple times.

As it played, his eyes flickered back and forth between his notes and the transcript on his computer screen. The voice on the other end of the line was panicked, barely intelligible.

Please, you have to come help us! My friend...something terrible happened to her—I think she's dead... I don't know what to do!

To Grayson, the roommate's call raised some questions. Kathy didn't immediately identify herself, only doing so after repeated requests from the dispatcher for her name. She also didn't mention Goins's name during the call that lasted nearly eight minutes. She described the body she had come upon only as her friend.

Then there was the moment that Kathy was reluctant to touch the victim's body despite repeated pleas from the dispatcher to see if Melanie was still breathing.

"How was the roommate acting when you arrived on the scene?" he asked.

"When I got there, Kathy was near hysterics," Charlie said. "She eventually had to be taken to the hospital and given a sedative. Walking into her apartment and finding her friend like that...it had to be traumatizing."

Grayson gave a slight nod. "I see from your notes that you briefly considered her a suspect."

"I did," Charlie responded. "It just seemed a little convenient to me that she forgot to lock the door when she left the apartment. She said that she'd been drinking that night and must have forgotten to lock it when she left. Kathy seemed genuinely broken up over Melanie's death and blamed herself. From all accounts, they were very close—there wasn't motive. But then she showed a different side after Melanie's funeral. It was after that, that I was told Kathy and Melanie's relationship was turbulent in the months leading up to her death." Giving him a hard stare, she stated, "I guess you think I didn't know how to do my job."

"Charlie, I wasn't thinking that at all."

He knew she was looking for a fight and he wasn't going to give her one. Grayson leaned back in his chair, tapping his pen thoughtfully against his notepad. The case was proving to be a bit more complex than he originally anticipated. He couldn't shake the feeling that something wasn't right—that there was more to Melanie's death than what was in front of them.

"So, what are your initial thoughts?" she asked.

"I think we need to look deeper into the victim's personal life," he said, breaking the tense silence. "Perhaps she had enemies or someone who held a grudge against her."

"During the initial investigation, I went through Melanie's social media accounts and her phone. I spoke with her professors at the university. She had been a popular student, and just about everybody I talked to spoke highly of her character. Her sorority sisters talked animatedly about how hard she studied or the fun times they shared together."

"You mentioned that you're part of the same sorority, didn't you?" he asked.

"Yes, I did," she replied, sounding slightly defensive. "But that doesn't mean I'm biased in any way."

"Charlie, I'm not implying anything," Grayson said. "I just noticed that the bracelet you're wearing has the same emblem as the one on this pillow in the crime scene photo."

"It was a gift from one of my line sisters. I haven't been active much since I graduated college. Anyway, we're not talking about my life," she stated. "Our focus is on Melanie Goins and finding her killer."

"Yes, ma'am." Grayson couldn't help but feel intrigued by learning Charlie was part of a sorority. He had known her for years and never would have guessed it. He always assumed Charlie preferred her own company. She was a loner.

However, now wasn't the time to try to figure out his new partner. They had a case to solve.

When their meeting ended, Charlie walked back to her desk, her mind replaying the conversation she'd just had with Grayson. So often in the past he'd been disruptive and arrogant—trying to prove he was the expert and better than everybody else—but today he was so much more considerate. He'd waited patiently for her to get her theories about the murder out, and she was struck by how different he seemed from his usual self.

She was the one acting defensive and on edge. Charlie told herself that there wasn't any need for her to feel so insecure around Grayson. She reminded herself that she'd earned the right to be in the CCU—the same as he had. Charlie hadn't thought he'd be returning to the unit after the accident. There was a time when she respected Grayson, even nurtured an attraction to him, but then he went behind her back to their supervisor about the way she was handling her first case.

When her gaze lingered too long on his strong features, Charlie reminded herself that this was the same man who had thrown her under the bus to make a name for himself, only now they were partners.

Charlie sat down at her desk and tried to focus on her work, but her thoughts kept drifting back to Grayson.

She had caught a glimpse of the new Grayson. He was

patient and considerate, but still a man who was passionate about his work. A man who was also undeniably attractive.

Every time she looked up into his strong features, Charlie felt torn between her resentment toward what he'd done and the admiration for how far he'd come in his career. Her respect for him had diminished and yet, there was still something about him that attracted her. But the truth was that Charlie could never trust him.

Charlie had built walls around her heart to protect herself and buried herself in books; the world in them was something she could control. When people tried to break down the barriers around her heart, she felt vulnerable. Though she longed for comfort and connection, she'd become so accustomed to having to rely solely on herself. There was only one person she considered a friend. Jen Wells, a sergeant II in the robbery unit.

She stole a peek over to Grayson's workspace. He was involved in a deep conversation with the detective seated across from him. From the tidbits she overheard, they were discussing a case. Grayson was considered one of the top criminal investigators in the homicide unit and also in the CCU. Charlie acknowledged that she could learn a lot from him, but her past experience with him wounded her deeply and she refused to let history repeat itself. She was new to the CCU and intended to prove herself on the two cases she was currently investigating. She had no intentions of letting Grayson take lead on the Goins case.

When Phillipa walked past her desk, she made a mental note to stop at a store after work to purchase a wedding gift.

Charlie sighed. She wasn't looking forward to attending Phillipa and Kyle's nuptials. It just wasn't her thing.

As she got up from her desk to grab a fresh cup of coffee, Charlie couldn't help but think about how much she disliked all the pomp and grandeur of weddings. The forced socializing and the uncomfortable formal wear made her want to hide out in her home.

Charlie walked toward the break room, catching sight of Phillipa in the hallway talking with another female officer. The bride-to-be was positively beaming, with a huge grin plastered across her face. Charlie couldn't help but feel a pang of jealousy at how happy Phillipa looked. Charlie knew she would never find someone to love and spend the rest of her life with—she'd made peace with being alone.

She shook her head and pushed the thoughts aside. She didn't have time to start feeling sorry for herself.

After leaving the precinct, Grayson wandered through the department store, his hands in his pockets as he studied the contents of each aisle. The air smelled like a mixture of perfume, scented candles and artisan soaps. A chorus of conversations echoed off the high ceilings of the building.

He paused at an aisle full of items for the home. Grayson's stomach churned with anxiety as he thought of his supervisor's upcoming wedding—he wanted to show Phillipa and Kyle how much he appreciated them both. He wanted to find something special.

As he made his way to the registry section, Grayson's mind raced with ideas. But he also knew he had to stay within his budget. The six-month medical leave had put somewhat of a dent in his finances, so he was careful with his spending. He finally settled on a set of luxurious bed sheets, carefully picking the right size and color that he knew they would love. It was on their wish list.

As he made his way to the checkout, a voice caught his attention. "Grayson, is that you?" He turned around to see his ex-girlfriend, a former detective on the force who left to pursue a career in journalism.

"Hey, Lacey," Grayson said.

"I heard about your car accident. I have to say that you look like you're doing well."

"I had a rough patch right after. Months of physical therapy."

Lacey's eyes softened with empathy.

Grayson smiled. "Yeah, it was tough. But I'm still here and healthy. How have you been?"

Lacey shrugged. "Can't complain. I'm still at the paper, chasing down leads and writing stories. It's not as exciting as being a detective, but it pays the bills."

Grayson nodded, feeling a sense of admiration for Lacey. She was always so determined and focused, even when the odds were against her. "That's great. Any interesting stories lately?"

Lacey's expression grew serious. "Actually, I'm starting a new chapter. I'm getting married."

"Congratulations," he said.

"I'm still trying to process this whole thing myself. Everything happened so fast."

"I'm happy for you."

She eyed him. "Grayson, are you really happy for me?"

He cleared his throat and smiled. "Of course, Lacey. I'm thrilled for you. Who's the lucky guy?"

Her face lit up with a smile. "His name is Edward. He's an investigative reporter, and we met at a conference in Los Angeles eight months ago. We hit it off instantly, and we've been inseparable ever since."

Lacey deserved happiness even if it was with someone other than him. "He sounds like a great guy," Grayson said.

"He is," she replied with a smile.

On his way out of the store, Grayson noticed Charlie.

Their eyes locked and held.

She appeared surprised at seeing him and he mirrored her surprise.

"Looks like we both had the same idea," Grayson commented, breaking the silence between them. "Phillipa and Kyle are registered here—I don't know what I would've done without that information."

"Same here," Charlie agreed.

"Well, I'll see you tomorrow at the station then," Grayson said.

"Have a good night," Charlie said after throwing him a stiff nod.

Grayson watched her go. Although he had always found her attractive, he vowed to never act on it. Resolutely shaking his head, he chased the thoughts away. He didn't doubt that after they closed the Goins case, they would most likely find ways to avoid one another.

THREE

Charlie stood there, staring blankly at the wedding gift registry in her hands. She hated stuff like this. She considered just buying a random gift card. She couldn't help but feel a sense of resentment boil up within her. Charlie was tired of attending these weddings: endless hours spent listening to speeches, making conversation with people she didn't want to talk to—it all felt so contrived.

She let out a sigh, feeling the weight of the registry in her hands. As Charlie flipped through the pages, her eyes lingered on a particular item, a set of handmade ceramic mugs. They were beautiful, with delicate navy-blue patterns painted on the surface.

The thought of wrapping her hands around one of those mugs, sipping hot cocoa on a cold winter night, sounded blissful. She imagined herself cozied up on the couch, the mug warming her hands as she lost herself in a good book.

She set her jaw firmly and came to a decision. Charlie was getting the mugs.

For herself.

With a silent sigh, Charlie realized that she still had to find something for Phillipa and Kyle.

After spending what seemed like an hour searching through

the housewares department, she finally settled on the decorative towels Kyle and Phillipa had put on their registry.

Charlie paid for her purchase and had them gift wrapped at the store.

As she walked out of the store, she couldn't shake the feeling of emptiness that had been growing inside her for some time. It wasn't just the wedding that was getting to her. The truth was, she was tired of feeling like a spectator in her own life, always going through the motions but never really living.

Charlie longed for something to break up the monotony of her everyday life. To give her purpose. It was the main reason why she decided to go into law enforcement. Focusing on solving crimes allowed her to take her mind off her own life for a while.

But as she drove home from the store, Charlie couldn't help but wonder if being a detective was enough. Working her cases was frustrating, but at least they were a good distraction. They kept her from focusing on her own problems.

The next day, Charlie sat at her desk, staring blankly at the computer screen in front of her. She had been working on another case for a couple weeks now, and it seemed like all the evidence was leading nowhere. Typically, she was able to find overlooked clues and solve mysteries without difficulty, but this case had her stumped and feeling helpless. She wasn't ready to give up though. She was determined to close this one and the Goins case, too.

Charlie leaned back in her chair; her eyes closed as she took several deep breaths to clear her mind. As she exhaled, her thoughts drifted back to her childhood and she felt her chest tighten.

Even though it was years ago, she could still remember the way her heart raced every time her parents fought, letting out drunken screams and hurling insults at each other. There were times when their anger was directed at her, their words tearing away chunks of her self-esteem and sense of security. When Child Protective Services took Charlie out of the home, she willed herself to never allow anyone to get close enough to hurt her ever again. Although her foster parents were loving and nurturing, Charlie remained guarded.

Her throat suddenly felt dry and she couldn't swallow; all Charlie wanted to do was curl up in a ball and disappear. Yet despite the heart ache that almost paralyzed her, she found the strength to stand up for herself and not let others define her. She opened her eyes and stared resolutely at the computer screen.

Charlie switched to the Goins case. She eyed the note. It had been sloppily written in ballpoint pen on what was believed to be the torn-off bottom of a white paper bag. CSI had determined the type was commonly used at fast-food restaurants. She believed that the bag may have come from Rodney's Burgers, located near the Charlotte University campus. The note didn't have a speck of blood on it, although the bedroom had blood splattered all around.

She turned her attention to the wine bottle. Her uncle was familiar with the brand and had informed her that it was only sold in Italy. He had no idea how she had acquired it, but assumed it must have been a gift or something Melanie had ordered for herself.

Suddenly, Charlie heard the clicking of heels as someone approached her desk. She looked up at her visitor.

"We're meeting in the break room at two to prepare for the shower. It's in the conference room" Jen said, keeping her voice down. It was supposed to be a surprise for Phillipa and Kyle.

"Can't I just give my gift to you?" Charlie asked. "I don't really do bridal showers."

"You always say that."

"That's because it's the truth."

"This is for Phillipa…your supervisor, so obviously you can't get out of it that easily."

Charlie let out an exasperated sigh. "Fine. But I have a lot of work to do so I won't be staying long."

"Girl, we *all* have a lot of work, or did you miss all those files stacked up on my desk?"

"You know what I mean, Jen."

"I'll see you at two."

She watched her friend walk to the next workstation, before pausing to talk to the detective seated there. Jen was most definitely a people person, a social butterfly. She loved parties and all social gatherings—everything Charlie hated. They were complete opposites but their friendship was solid.

Jen was the only person Charlie had allowed into her nonexistent circle. She was the only one who knew her secrets and had proven herself trustworthy.

Charlie bit her lip, and a cold sweat beaded on her brow as the clock ticked closer to the time of the bridal shower. She had spent years building walls between herself and other colleagues, shying away from any camaraderie, and she felt exposed at the prospect of having to put aside her defenses for even one afternoon.

The shower was held in a large conference room on the second floor. A banner was strung across, stretching from wall to wall and reading CONGRATULATIONS! The exquisite decor featured an elegant color scheme of emerald green and gold, with matching streamers and balloons hanging from the ceiling. A large buffet of food lined one table: cheeses, meats and breads of all kinds. On another was a variety of treats—from chocolates to cookies. The third table held a small wedding cake, cupcakes and drinks.

Charlie was greeted by her coworkers' smiling faces and couldn't help but feel a small flicker of warmth in her chest. Maybe they weren't all bad, she thought to herself. But she wasn't ready to completely let down her guard, despite Jen's best efforts. However, as the night wore on, Charlie found herself chatting with her colleagues in a way she never had before.

Grayson was noticeably absent during the shower, but he'd dropped off his gift. Charlie left as soon as she could, before returning to her desk.

"Hey, I just got off the phone with John Wheaton," he announced from his desk. "He's a forensic specialist I met a few years ago. He's going to send over his preliminary thoughts on the crime scene and evidence before the end of day."

Charlie offered him a smile of gratitude. "That's great. How did you convince him to move so fast."

"He owes me a favor," Grayson said. "How was the shower?"

"Everyone seemed to be having a great time."

"What about you?" he asked. "You have fun?"

"*Fun?* What's that?"

They both laughed.

Realizing that she'd let her guard down just a little, Charlie returned to professional mode. "I need to get back to work. I have another case that I'd like to get off my desk."

"I could take a look at it," Grayson offered. "That's if you'd like another perspective."

Charlie hesitated for a moment. She had always worked alone and was skeptical about involving Grayson in another investigation. But the case was convoluted, and she needed all the help she could get. Charlie rationalized that letting him help her with this case would reveal if he was really a changed man. Wanting to see if he would betray her a second time, she walked over and handed Grayson the file.

"It's a complex case," Charlie warned.

Grayson flipped through the pages, analyzing each detail with his sharp eyes. She couldn't deny that he had always been good at reading between the lines, and that's what made him a great detective.

"Interesting," he muttered after a moment. "My gut instinct tells me that this looks like a classic case of murder-for-hire."

Charlie raised an eyebrow. "What makes you say that?"

"I'm familiar with the victim from my street patrol days. Hendrix had a history of getting into trouble with the wrong people before he turned his life around. Instinct tells me that his death was made to look like his past had finally caught up to him." Grayson looked up at her. "The one who stood to gain the most was who?"

"His wife," she responded.

He pointed to a photograph. "This is the best friend, right?"

Charlie nodded before taking a seat in the empty chair in front of his desk.

"Check out the photos of him and the widow."

She looked up at him. "They're together…"

Grayson pointed to one photograph in particular. "This was taken by one of the news outlets."

"They do look really cozy in this one," Charlie said. "But if you read his statement, you'll see that he had a solid alibi for the night the victim was shot."

"I never said he committed the crime. Just that he stood to gain from it." Grayson pulled up the man's social media page. "Let's see if we can find some photographs before the victim died."

"He posted a moving tribute to Hendrix the day after he died," Charlie said. She had already checked out his social pages.

Grayson nodded and pointed. "Now this picture was posted six weeks after the death of his friend. He bought a luxury car and then he starts wearing expensive designer clothing. Look at the post with him flashing his brand-new watch."

"It's a Rolex or a good fake."

"I bet it's the real deal," he responded.

"So, you think he and the wife were lovers?"

"I do."

"And that he had his friend killed." Charlie nodded thoughtfully. "That's a good theory. But we'll need to find evidence. She's currently married to someone else and so is he. But now, I am really interested in learning where his money came from."

"Follow the money…"

"Grayson, thanks. Every lead I was following led to a dead end. Now that I think about it, they were all leads that he and Hendrix's wife had given me. I need to see if I can dismantle their alibis." Charlie stood up. "When I bring him in, I'd like for you to be there when I interview him."

"Sure. Anytime."

He didn't attempt to persuade her into letting him work the case with her. Grayson offered his theory and that was all. She gave him a genuine smile before walking across the floor to her workstation. She sat down to make several phone calls.

Charlie had been so focused on her task that she hadn't noticed that it was close to the end of her shift until she looked up and saw Grayson, still deep in Melanie Goins's murder book. They were going to reconvene tomorrow once he'd read through all the documentation from eighteen months of investigation. There was a lot of information to go over.

This was the case he wanted, she thought as a wave of insecurity washed over her. This was *her* investigation.

Grayson cared about this one because it had been such a high-profile case back then. He needed something like this to give his career the jolt it required after his six-month absence. But Charlie wasn't about to let him snatch this case from her, which meant that she had to stay on top of every ounce of information and evidence that came across her desk.

She got up from her desk, grabbing the printed documents and shoving them into her burgundy tote bag. She slung it over her shoulder, giving Grayson a curt wave before heading briskly toward the exit doors. He was on his best behavior and trying not do anything that might upset her. Despite this, Charlie intended to keep her guard up; all their interactions so far had been civil but that didn't mean she trusted him.

Thirty minutes later, Charlie sat at a coffee shop near her house, sipping on chai tea, as she flipped through the pages of the newspaper. The article about a missing young woman found dead had her clenching her fists in anger. It was stories like these that reminded her of her own trauma.

Charlie put down the newspaper and pulled out her iPad, before jotting down new questions regarding the Goins investigation while they were still fresh in her mind.

It still galled her that Grayson had been assigned to work the investigation with her. The truth was that she wouldn't have been thrilled with anyone. She didn't like working with partners. For now, she had to play nice, at least for the sake of the case.

Charlie checked the time on her watch. As the coffee shop started to fill up with people, she grabbed her tote and stood quickly. She couldn't stand the thought of being around such a large crowd in such a small space.

As she made her way through the doors, Charlie breathed a sigh of relief. The fresh air was a welcome change from the claustrophobic atmosphere of the shop. She walked briskly to her car in the parking lot, pondering how she hoped to spend her evening: rereading witness statements and interviews.

Charlie was determined not to let Melanie down again.

When she arrived home, Charlie entered her house from the garage.

In the family room, she glanced over at the row of shelves that held her cherished collection of Native American pottery. The bright colors and intricate patterns seemed to shimmer in the evening light.

Charlie smiled as she drifted closer, her fingertips tracing the shapes etched into the clay.

Since discovering the Cherokee Art Market during a visit to North Carolina a few months ago, she had become obsessed with adding new pieces to her collection.

On the wall above was an amethyst dream catcher that was gifted to her by her sorority sisters. She didn't believe in the myths surrounding them—she liked it because it was her favorite color and was a gift.

Charlie went upstairs and settled in her bedroom. She spread her files across her king-size bed, then crawled into the middle. It was time to get back to work. At home, she could focus more without all the distractions of people milling around the precinct.

The next day, Grayson arrived at the precinct early, determined to get a head start on his work before his meeting with Charlie. He had some questions about the witnesses, among other things. He was eager to take on the Goins case, convinced that it would prove he was still fit for the job. But working with Charlie initially posed a challenge Grayson wasn't sure he could meet. She had always been confrontational and was notorious for not getting along well with others. She was a tough nut to crack, but despite her abrasive personality, Charlie was a dedicated detective. Though Grayson felt apprehensive about having to collaborate with her, he vowed to do his best to get along in order to solve the Goins murder.

He had always been overconfident, even felt superior to some of his coworkers until he was involved in that devastating car accident. His brush with death forced Grayson to rethink his life and consider what God's plan for him might be. During his recovery, he devoted much time to talking to God and reading the Bible. His experience changed his outlook on life, and he knew without a doubt that it was God who had saved him.

Charlie arrived thirty minutes ahead of her start time. She went to the break room for a cup of coffee, then gestured for him to join her as she made her way to an empty conference room.

"Since we're going over the witness statements this morning, I'd like to know more about Melanie's roommate… Kathy Dixon," Grayson said as soon as they sat down. "I want to know everything you know about her."

"It's like I told you… Melanie and Kathy were always described as close friends," Charlie said. "Kathy told me that Melanie helped her get a restraining order against her former boyfriend. She referred to the victim as her sister from another mother."

"Would you leave your *sister* at home with the door unlocked?" he asked.

"I wouldn't leave anyone without locking the door, but that's just me," Charlie responded. "That was one of the first things I asked her. I wanted to know if she had her keys on her or if she'd left them at the apartment. Kathy said that she took them with her. She claimed she forgot to lock the door—they had been drinking earlier at the club."

"They were underage."

"Fake IDs," Charlie responded. "That club was closed a few weeks later for serving alcohol to minors."

Grayson scanned the statement, then said, "Kathy told you that the reason they left the club was because she wasn't feeling well."

Charlie nodded. "Correct."

"But two hours later, she leaves the apartment to spend the night with a friend. Did she drive or was she picked up?"

"She took her car," she responded.

"She then returns the next morning to find the victim dead in the apartment. Outside of the obvious shock, grief and trauma…what were your observations when you interviewed her?" he asked.

"She was very emotional from the trauma of seeing Melanie like that—nervous and jittery. It was consistent with anyone who had walked in to find a dead body. I felt she was credible initially."

"What happened to change your mind about her?"

"I went to Melanie's funeral. Kathy seemed like a different person. Not a hint of emotion. She showed no signs of grief. She was truly a chatty Kathy—not withdrawn or quiet like I expected. Then there was my conversation with the victim's former roommate, Spring Whitefeather. She mentioned that Kathy had been acting incredibly paranoid, constantly checking her phone and looking over her shoulder since the murder. Another friend told me that Kathy had been drinking heavily the night before the funeral."

"Sounds like the ex-roommate believed Kathy had something to do with Melanie's death," Grayson stated.

Charlie nodded. "Oh, Spring was very vocal about it. She went as far as to mention that Kathy never left the door unlocked before. I got the impression that the two women didn't like one another. Spring then told me that there had been some discord between Kathy and Melanie.

"Roommates argue, so it didn't come as a surprise to me. But the way Spring described Kathy after the murder... it prompted me to give her a second look. I wanted to consider every avenue."

"Did anyone else you talked to try to turn the spotlight on Kathy?" he asked. "Or could jealousy have been the motive for Spring?"

"According to Spring, Kathy was jealous of her relationship with Melanie," Charlie responded. "For all I know, it could've been the other way around. I had to also consider that maybe Spring didn't like that Melanie chose to move in with Kathy. But nothing gave me a solid reason for either of them to want the victim dead."

Frowning in confusion, Grayson said, "I don't know... I'm really trying to understand why Kathy would leave her roommate at home with the door unlocked like that."

"I don't drink, but I've been around people who do," Charlie responded. "It's possible she simply forgot to lock the door."

"If she was that drunk, why did she get behind the wheel of her car?" Grayson clenched his jaw in anger as he thought, *How could she have been so reckless? How could she have taken such an unnecessary risk?* He was all too aware of the danger of driving while intoxicated, having himself been hit by a drunk driver and barely escaping death.

"Kathy admitted that she shouldn't have been driving but said her friend lived five minutes away."

He picked up one of the crime scene photos, a wave of sadness washing over him. "Who did this to you?" he whispered.

"I intend to find out," Charlie said. "That woman didn't deserve to die like that. No one does."

FOUR

On Saturday afternoon, Charlie ran her fingers through her freshly cropped hair and admired herself in the bathroom mirror without makeup. As she walked into her bedroom, she struggled with what to wear—a dressy pantsuit or a cocktail dress. She was leaning toward the suit but thought the dress might be more fitting for the occasion.

Her gaze settled on the shoebox of nude heels and she tried to recall when she last wore them. In her mind's eye, she envisioned herself slipping and stumbling as she walked up to her seat in front of all those people.

Charlie shook away the thought.

I'm not going to be negative.

It was Phillipa and Kyle's wedding. Although Charlie wasn't a people person, she really liked them. This was the only reason she was attending their nuptials. She opted for the strapless dress with a subtle neckline, the A-line silhouette hugging her waist and flaring out at her hips.

The hem of the luxurious sapphire garment swept gracefully around her knees.

"I'm as ready as I'm gonna be," she whispered. If she didn't leave in the next few minutes, she risked being late.

Charlie nearly tripped on her way out the door. She was tempted to take off her heels, but she didn't have any other shoes to compliment her dress. Taking her time, she made her way to the car and was soon on her way.

She arrived with ten minutes to spare.

Inside, the sanctuary smelled of scented candles and fresh flowers. Vivid colors of gold, green, purple and red in the stained-glass windows cast a bejeweled light in the church. The wooden pews looked as if they'd been polished for the ceremony.

Charlie considered they might always look like that—this was her first time visiting this church. It had been years since she'd attended services anywhere. There was no need because she'd abandoned her faith a long time ago when God chose not to rescue her from dire circumstances.

She pasted on a smile as she joined her coworkers who were seated together.

"You look great," Jen whispered. "I love that dress on you."

"Thank you," she responded, then added, "So do you."

Charlie couldn't help but notice Grayson as he entered the sanctuary, dressed in a dark navy expensive-looking suit. He was quite handsome. As the music came to life and the ceremony began, Charlie tried to push her thoughts of Grayson away to focus on the moment.

The bridesmaids glided down the aisle, wearing shimmering gold dresses. Phillipa's daughter and Kyle's twin nieces were much younger than the other attendants, but they looked just as beautiful in their emerald-green gowns.

The music changed to a slow, romantic melody. The crowd turned their attention to the back of the church, where the bride appeared, arm in arm with her father. Phillipa looked stunning in a pale gold wedding gown as she slowly made her way down the aisle.

Charlie watched as Phillipa's father gave her a loving kiss on the cheek, then placed her hand into Kyle's. A part of her was happy for them, but another part of her couldn't help but feel a profound sense of sadness; she would never know what it was like to share such a special moment with her own dad. Charlie had no idea where he could be or even if he was still alive—she had never even tried to find him. Her mother had died shortly after she graduated high school.

The couple turned to face each other, their eyes locked in a loving gaze.

"Phillipa looks so beautiful," Jen whispered.

Charlie nodded, trying to hide the envy that threatened to overwhelm her. She was truly glad for Kyle and Phillipa, surrounded by people who had always been so supportive of them, yet a nagging feeling tugged at her heart, reminding Charlie of how lonely she felt deep down and how she had never managed to find anything remotely close to the kind of connection they shared.

After the ceremony, Charlie slipped out of the pew intent on skipping the reception and going home.

"Do you mind if I ride with you to the hotel?" Jen asked, walking beside her.

"I'm going home," she replied, her tone unwavering.

Jen stared at her incredulously. "Charlie…the reception is the best part of a wedding. Don't you want to celebrate? C'mon now…"

"Fine," she reluctantly agreed. "I can drop you off."

Jen released an audible sigh. "Charlie, why do you insist on pushing people away and being so antisocial? You need companionship in this world. It's not healthy to be alone all the time."

Charlie looked away, her expression unreadable. "I'm just not a people person," she finally stated. "You know that."

Jen sighed again. "Charlie, I know you're not a people person," she said, her voice gentle. "But you can't keep shutting everyone out. You're going to regret it one day."

Charlie didn't reply, and the entire car ride was silent.

Eventually, they arrived at the hotel where the reception was being held.

Jen got out of the car. "Thanks for the ride, beautiful."

Charlie watched her go before letting out a deep sigh and parking in an empty space.

When she walked into the hotel lobby, she found Jen standing there, waiting with a grin on her face.

"Just don't say a word," Charlie uttered.

"Thank you for staying," Jen said.

"I just hope I don't regret it."

The reception was beautiful, the flowers vibrant and the decorations elegant. Everyone was having a good time. Charlie was sitting alone, watching the crowd. She saw Phillipa and Kyle dancing together, lost in the moment.

Charlie was there, but her mind was elsewhere. She regretted allowing Jen to talk her into staying because she was bored. She would much rather be at home barefoot, dressed in a pair of too-big sweatpants and a T-shirt, working her cases.

The food was delicious and she'd been hungry. Now that she had a full stomach, Charlie saw no point in hanging out any longer. She had spent some time chatting with her coworkers, had even allowed Jen to drag her onto the dance floor to the tune of Beyoncé's "Single Ladies." She drew a hard line against line dancing, mostly because she didn't know the moves and wasn't in the mood to learn.

Charlie's gaze darted around the room, but it was constantly drawn back to Grayson. He appeared to be having a great time, talking and laughing with other guests at his table, while Phillipa and Kyle had managed to mingle their coworkers with different groups.

Meanwhile, Charlie and Jen had been fortunate to be seated at the same table. While her other tablemates were out on the dance floor or busy talking to other people, Charlie was left alone with her thoughts. She tried to focus on anything else, but she couldn't help stealing glances at Grayson.

What are you doing?

Charlie didn't have an answer, so she dismissed it totally. She glanced down at the watch on her arm. She would give it another fifteen minutes or so before leaving. She wanted to get back to finding the people responsible for both the Hendrix and Goins murders.

In all the years he'd known her, Grayson had never seen Charlie in a dress before now. She had the legs of a runner, muscled and toned. She looked nice…no, make that stunning. He considered going over to say hello to her but thought better of it. He didn't want her snapping at him in front of their coworkers or the other wedding guests.

As he continued to observe Charlie from afar, Grayson couldn't help but feel a strange pull toward her. He didn't want to sit there and pretend she wasn't a few feet away from his table. He debated with himself for a few moments, unsure of what to do. Finally, he decided to take a chance and walk over to her.

"Charlie," Grayson said, his voice barely above a whisper.

She turned to face him, her eyes narrowing. "What do you want?" she asked, her tone cold and distant. "I hope you didn't come over here to ask me to dance."

Grayson took a deep breath before saying, "Actually, I came to talk."

Charlie raised an eyebrow, studying him. "Oh."

He sat down in the empty chair beside her. "I keep thinking about the Goins case."

"So do I," she responded. "I've gone over everything so many times—I think I have it memorized by now."

"I've had a couple cases like that in the past. I review them every few years to see if I can figure out the missing pieces. Nothing irks me more than to have a case go cold. I take it personally."

"Is that why you transferred to the CCU?" Charlie asked.

Grayson nodded. "Yeah. I want to be able to give the families of these victims some answers. I figured I could do the most good in this department."

"You and I have something in common."

"Imagine that," he said with a smile.

"Don't get carried away," Charlie responded, her tone dry. "I'm sure most of the people we work with feel the same way. It's not a big deal."

"Why do you dislike me so much?" It was something he had wanted to ask her for a long time. Grayson hoped he was prepared for the answer.

His question seemed to surprise her. After a moment, Charlie said, "I always knew you were a narcissist. You were a know-it-all and acted like you were better than everybody else, but when you had my case taken away—I knew you couldn't be trusted."

"I didn't set out to take over that case," he responded.

"What did you think would happen after you went complaining about me? You were the darling of the homicide unit. You could do no wrong. What really angered me was that you were supposed to be my mentor. You have no idea how hard it was to go to you in the first place. I really wanted to work my case alone. I wanted to prove myself to Captain Jamison."

"That's not exactly how it happened," Grayson said. "Jamison asked me how things were going and I was honest. I mentioned not only your weak areas, but also your strengths. I never expected Jamison to yank you off the investigation. I even tried to get him to change his mind. But you know Jamison—he wanted headlines. He wanted someone with more experience."

"He never liked me," Charlie stated.

"No, he didn't," Grayson agreed. "Jamison didn't like a lot of people. That's part of the reason he's no longer with the department."

"That was my very first homicide case. You have no idea how it felt to have to hand it over to you. You can try to deny it but I know you were thrilled to be the one who'd solved it."

"I guess that was the old me," he replied. "But I'm no longer that person."

"What happened to you?" she asked. "Why the change?"

"Nearly dying can do that to a person."

"I saw the photos from your accident. It's amazing you survived, Grayson. For what it's worth… I'm glad you're still among the living."

He smiled. "I didn't think you cared."

She laughed. "I know people don't believe it, but I do have a heart. I wouldn't wish death on anyone."

Grayson stole glances at Charlie. He felt drawn to her, even though he couldn't explain why.

"So, what's the plan of action?" he asked after a moment.

"I think we should interview all the witnesses again," she said, changing the direction of their conversation. "See if any of their stories have changed."

He nodded in agreement. "People tend to remember things differently over time. I'm especially interested in hearing what Spring Whitefeather and Kathy Dixon have to say."

"Me, too." Charlie rose to her feet. "I'm about to head out. I want to go back over the list of witnesses."

"If you'd like, we can continue our discussion at the precinct," Grayson said.

"Sure. I'll follow you there. We can use one of the empty offices to lay out the case."

"You don't want to go home and change?" he asked. "Your shoes are nice but they don't look that comfortable."

"I have some stuff in my car. I can change at the precinct."

"Always prepared, I see."

Charlie offered him a rare smile. "I try to be. I don't like surprises."

Charlie breathed a sigh of relief after she'd changed into jeans and a comfortable shirt. Her feet were very forgiving now that they were enclosed in a pair of sneakers.

She joined Grayson in an empty office. He was still dressed in his suit but had removed his tie and unbuttoned the top two buttons. An old-fashioned wooden desk stood in the center. Two chairs were pushed against one wall while a whiteboard filled the far wall. "Okay, let's get started," she stated as she sat down at the desk.

Grayson pulled up one of the visitor chairs and followed suit.

"Kathy's ex-boyfriend Cisco Jenner was there at the club the night of Melanie's death," he said, holding up a document. "I thought I read that Kathy had a restraining warrant against him."

"She did, but it had expired by then," Charlie responded. "He was at the club with a date. No one ever saw him speak to Kathy or Melanie. His attention was on the person he was with. When I interviewed Cisco right after the murder, he didn't have anything nice to say about either woman. Yet, there were text messages on his phone from Kathy the previous day."

"Yeah, I thought that was interesting, too," he said. "What was her explanation?"

"Kathy claimed that she'd texted Cisco because she wanted to return some jewelry belonging to him that she'd found at the apartment."

"Why do you think he kept texting back, Who is this?"

"I don't know but I can still feel the frost after all these years. He was almost kicked out of the university because of the restraining order," Charlie said. "I'm not sure I'd be all that forgiving if I were in his shoes."

Laying the document on the desk, Grayson responded, "Sounds like a motive to me. Melanie was the person who convinced Kathy to get the restraining order in the first place. She said that he blamed Melanie for their breakup."

"His date was his alibi for that night. She said that he spent the night at her place."

"Let's see if she still remembers it that way," he suggested.

Charlie nodded in agreement.

"I think we should also talk to the former neighbors. Tabitha Raines, Valerie Nobles and Lucas Shelby. To see if they remember anything else about that night." Grayson stood up and made his way to the whiteboard. Using a black marker, he wrote down the names of everyone they wanted to interview.

He returned to his seat when he finished. "This unknown witness…"

Slowly twirling the pen with her finger, Charlie said, "Two weeks after Melanie's death, someone emailed the precinct and said they knew who killed her. We traced it to a coffee bar near the university."

"Any video?"

"Nope. Unfortunately, I never heard anything else," she responded. "The manager of the shop said he gets lots of students coming in and out of the place and a few businesspeople who work in the area as well. He said it could be any of his customers. However, around the time that email was sent, it could have most likely been a college student." It still irked Charlie that she hadn't been able to identify the sender.

"I read the email. Maybe they were in one of her classes or lived in the same apartment building. Then there's the possibility that they are not a witness but a suspect."

"I considered that," she responded. "Maybe it's why we never heard anything else from the person. Maybe they had a moment of guilt and wanted to confess, but then changed their mind."

Grayson got up. "I'm going to list this person as an unknown suspect for now."

Charlie agreed. "My gut is telling me that they just may be the missing piece. We find them—we just might get the answers we need to close this case."

"Tobias Jacobs…"

"Jacobs was a student at the university. He and Melanie had gone out twice and had been texting back and forth. He consented to a DNA swab but didn't want to continue talking to me. The only thing he told me is that he'd met Melanie a few weeks before her death. Other than the two dates and seeing her on campus, Tobias claimed he didn't know much about the victim. They were just starting to build a friendship before she was killed."

"I see that you ruled him out as a person of interest."

"Yes," Charlie responded. "The same with Alfonso Levy. He was another university student. He danced with Melanie that night at the club. He also told me that he didn't know her very well. Just saw her on campus from time to time. Levy also consented to a DNA swab. Neither he nor Jacobs was a match to any of the DNA found at the scene. They also weren't wine drinkers. Tobias said he was a beer type of man and Alfonso believed in clean living. He didn't drink."

"I'd still like to talk to them," Grayson said. "Recollections vary, but there may be something they remember now that they didn't back then." He added them to his list.

"I don't think we're going to get much from Tobias Jacobs, but it's worth a shot. Back then, I really thought the $30,000 reward would bring this case to a close quickly."

"I remember when it was announced," he responded. The Cherokee tribe, the university's board of trustees and the Crime Stoppers chapter had all donated the money. "I closed three cases after a reward was offered for information."

"Grayson, it's time to close this case. Nearly eleven years have passed since Melanie Goins was denied justice and I won't let her be forgotten." Charlie's voice echoed with intensity as she looked straight into Grayson's eyes, her face set in a hard, determined stare. "We must find closure for her and her family."

"I want the same thing as you," he responded.

"You want another win under your belt," Charlie stated. "It's more than that for me."

"I told you that I'm not that man anymore."

She met his gaze. "Sure, you say that now, Grayson."

"I mean it. I almost died six months ago, Charlie. I want my life to mean more than my name in newspapers."

"Grayson, despite having to work with you—I haven't forgotten how you burned me. Just know that you won't get a second chance."

FIVE

He felt the weight of Charlie's words hit him like a ton of bricks. He could see that Charlie had been deeply affected by Jamison's actions during their homicide days. Back then, Charlie had a few hiccups, the same as any new detective, but she'd earned her position and while she could be a pain to work with, she genuinely cared about the victims.

Grayson took a deep breath. "Charlie, I'm really sorry about what happened. It really wasn't my intent to take that case from you."

"We can't undo the past," she responded.

"You're right, but I want you to know that I've always been on your side."

Charlie shrugged in nonchalance. It was clear that she didn't believe him.

"Let's just get back to this investigation," she said.

"It's getting late," Grayson responded. "Let's call it a night. I have to come back here first thing in the morning. I hate working Sundays."

"I'm off tomorrow. So, on Monday morning, we'll start working this list." Charlie glanced at her watch. "Oh wow. I hadn't realized that we've been here for going on four hours." She stood up, gathering her files and preparing to leave the office.

Grayson felt a sense of dread wash over him. He knew how much this case meant to her. He had been down this road countless times before, and many times, the trail always seemed to go cold. But this time, something in Charlie's eyes told him that they were going to find the answers they had been searching for. They were going to find the person responsible for Melanie's death, no matter how long it took.

When Charlie got to the office on Monday morning, the first thing she did was call Kathy Dixon, the victim's former roommate.

"My last name is now Ross. I got married three years ago," she said after Charlie identified herself. "Did you finally find the person who killed Melanie?"

"Actually, this is why I'm calling. We're reopening the case and I'd like to go over the events leading to her death once more."

"Of course, if you think it'll help, but it's been almost eleven years… I'm not sure how well I remember. Although some things I will never forget, like finding her body."

"Do you mind coming down to the precinct to talk with me and my partner?" Charlie inquired.

There was a brief pause before she answered, "When did you have in mind? My daughter has a doctor's appointment at 10:00 a.m."

"Do you have a sitter or someone to watch her around two o'clock this afternoon?"

"My mother lives with us, so that won't be a problem," Kathy responded.

"Thank you," Charlie said. "We'll see you at 2:00 p.m."

She got up and strolled over to Grayson's desk. "The roommate is coming here at two. I can't wait to hear your thoughts on Mrs. Dixon-Ross."

"Great," he responded. "I spoke to the neighbor that lived below them…Tabitha Raines…she still lives in that same building. Tabitha is expecting us within the hour. She recently had surgery on her foot, so she asked that we come to her place."

They walked over to a dark gray vehicle, a Buick.

"Who's driving?" Charlie asked, then quickly added, "Grayson, I didn't mean that the way it sounded."

He chuckled nervously. "If you're more comfortable behind the wheel, go ahead."

She eyed him warily. "Just so you know, I'm aware that the accident wasn't your fault. I want you to know that I'm not at all hesitant to get into a car with you."

"Same ol' Charlie…" Grayson said with a chuckle.

He opened the driver-side door for her and she climbed inside before he walked around the car and got into the front passenger seat.

Charlie started the car. The engine purred to life, and they drove out of the precinct parking lot.

It was only a fifteen-minute drive to the apartment, which was situated near Charlotte University and nestled in the heart of the Queen City. The campus was a long horizontal stripe across the city, its manicured lawns and clean walkways, brick buildings and stately dorms all in perfect symmetry. The privately funded school was small with enrollment just over four thousand.

They drove past the trees and underbrush surrounding a rectangular edifice of concrete and steel. A few buildings were designed in an old-world style, but most of the architecture was modern, with solid lines and flat roofs that peered over the trees.

They pulled into the parking lot of the Alexander Apartments. The complex was surrounded by lush trees, giving them a cozy, homey feeling. The exterior was a bright yellow color with navy blue trim and balconies on each floor. As they made their way to Tabitha's apartment, the sound of loud laughter drifted down the stairway.

"I can't believe she still lives here," Charlie said. It was a stone's throw from the university and most of the residents were college students. "I couldn't do it."

"Some people hate change," he responded.

Charlie knocked on the door.

There was a bit of a lag between the knock and Tabitha actually opening the door. Charlie noticed the bandage on her foot and the crutches.

"Thank you for seeing us, Miss Raines," Grayson said, taking a seat in the living room.

Charlie sat down beside him.

Tabitha made a grimace as she eased down onto the sofa. After she was settled, she smiled. "I told Detective Tesarkee when she first came to my door after Melanie was found that I don't know too much about what happened but I'm a night owl and was up late. I was watching television when I heard what sounded like arguing and loud noises coming from the apartment upstairs—it was as if they were moving furniture. At the time, I didn't think nothing of it because it wasn't a rare occurrence…especially when Kathy's old boyfriend used to be there. I hate to say it, but they argued a lot. I just thought it was them."

"You never complained about the noise?"

Smiling, Tabitha shook her head. "It's been twenty-five years since I graduated, but I remember what it was like to be in college, Detective. There was never any real trouble until…until poor Melanie was murdered."

Grayson looked at Charlie, who had a contemplative expression on her face. He knew that she was comparing what Tabitha had just said to the woman's initial statement.

"Miss Raines, if you don't mind, can you tell us a bit more about Kathy's ex-boyfriend?" Charlie asked. "You mentioned him during our first conversation and that he and Kathy seemed to argue a lot."

Tabitha nodded. "His name was Cisco, and he was always causing trouble. He had a temper. I remember this one time, I overheard him threaten Melanie when she tried to intervene. He said that he would kill her if she didn't stay out of his relationship."

Grayson glanced over at Charlie, who nodded. So far, Tabitha's statement was consistent with the one she made initially.

"I want you to think back. Do you remember hearing someone leaving or entering the apartment the night Melanie was killed?" Grayson asked.

"You mean aside from the noise from within the apartment?"

"Yes."

Tabitha shook her head. "No, I'm sorry. I don't remember. It's been a long time."

"Was Melanie close to any of the other neighbors?" Charlie inquired.

"She was friendly enough, I suppose. I'd see her talking to Valerie and her roommate Lucas… They lived right across from Melanie and Kathy. It was just…you know, neighborly stuff. We weren't what you'd call friends. I'm sorry there's not more that I can tell you."

"You were home alone the night of the incident?" Grayson asked.

"I was. I love Westerns, so it was just me and *Gunsmoke*. After that, I watched *Wagon Train*."

"One more question," Charlie said. "How did Melanie seem in the weeks leading up to her death? Did she seem nervous or anxious?"

Tabitha shook her head no. "I guess she seemed her usual self."

"We appreciate you taking time out to talk to us," Grayson said as they prepared to leave.

"It's my pleasure. Thank you for coming here," Tabitha responded, pointing to her bandaged foot.

"Her story hasn't changed. I verified that *Gunsmoke* and *Wagon Train* played on the Western channel that night," Charlie uttered as soon as they were back in the vehicle. "We can cross her off the list."

Grayson agreed. "I really want to hear what Kathy has to say after all this time."

"I tried to find a reason to make her a suspect back then, but couldn't. We'll see if it changes." Charlie was doubtful, but she was keeping an open mind.

Grayson kept glancing at his watch every few minutes, as Kathy Ross hadn't shown up yet. She was going on twenty minutes late. He was beginning to wonder if she'd changed her mind.

He stood up when he saw a woman walking briskly with Charlie toward one of the interview rooms and followed them.

"I apologize for my tardiness," Kathy said, breathing hard as she took a seat near the door. "Right when it was time for me to head here, I had an unexpected family emergency. I had to drop a change of clothing at the school for my bonus son. I don't like the word *stepson.* Anyway, he was playing around and spilled grape juice all over his shirt and pants."

Her gaze seemed to linger on him to the point where

Grayson turned his attention to Charlie, who replied, "That's quite alright. We appreciate you coming in. We won't take too much of your time."

"May I ask why you decided to reopen Melanie's case?" Kathy inquired once they were all seated. "On the phone you said you didn't have any new information."

"We're hoping that will change," Charlie responded. "I realize that it's been a long time, but I'd like you to tell us everything that happened on September 6."

"After our classes ended, Melanie and I went to the campus library to study. She was helping me with a paper I had to write. I think we stayed there until about midnight. We left there and went to our apartment. Melanie wanted to hang out so we went to this club called Secrets. All the students used to hang out there, especially since they'd let us come in and dance," Kathy said, her eyes traveling to Grayson. She gave him a flirty grin, then continued. "They weren't supposed to sell liquor to underage students, but Melanie and I had fake IDs. We danced until I started feeling bad. I sat down for a few minutes to see if it would pass. When it didn't, I told Melanie I wanted to go home."

"What time was this?" Grayson asked.

"I think it was shortly after midnight."

Charlie glanced over at him before questioning, "What happened when the two of you returned to your apartment?"

"A friend and I were texting back and forth while Melanie went to her room. I figured she had just gone to bed," Kathy said. "My friend was having boyfriend problems. She wanted me to come over to keep her from doing something stupid—even though I wasn't feeling the best, I left the apartment an hour later, and didn't return until around 11:00 a.m. the next day. I'd called Melanie several times that morning, but kept getting her voice mail. When I didn't see her on campus, I went home to check on her and that's when I found her." She squeezed her eyes shut at the memory.

"Did you make a habit of leaving your front door unlocked, especially since you knew you wouldn't be coming back for hours?" Grayson inquired. "I'm assuming you had your key on you, right? After all, you did drive to your friend's house."

Kathy's body stiffened and she looked defensive. "Detective, I didn't leave it unlocked on purpose. It was an oversight."

"Did you drink that night?"

"Yes," she responded. "This guy at the club bought me a couple drinks. I think he might have put something in them and that's why I got sick."

"This is the first time you mentioned that you think someone tampered with your drink," Charlie stated.

"I didn't think it back then," Kathy replied. "I was trying to process Melanie's death. I only came to that conclusion recently because this would explain why I started to feel unwell."

"Was Melanie also drinking?" Grayson asked.

Shaking her head, Kathy said, "No. She didn't want to risk Security catching us. She was afraid of getting kicked out of school. Melanie preferred to drink at home."

"And you weren't afraid of getting caught?"

She eyed Grayson for a moment before answering, "Not really because I was…careful." Kathy paused a moment, then asked, "Have you talked to Cisco Jenner already?"

"Not yet," Charlie responded.

"Why do you ask?" Grayson inquired.

"When Cisco and I broke up, he blamed Melanie, and was furious with her. But I'm not saying he had anything to do with her death."

"Then what are you implying?" he questioned.

"I… I just thought you might want to talk to him a second time." She looked over at Charlie and asked, "Am I a suspect or something?"

"We intend to speak to everyone, Kathy."

"Detective Tesarkee is correct," Grayson said. "I was just curious why you brought up Cisco."

"Like I said…he blamed Melanie for coming between us. She wasn't out to break us up, but after he kicked down my bedroom door—she convinced me that he had violent tendencies. Melanie didn't want to see me get hurt. I don't think he harmed her, but he might have heard something about what happened."

"From what I understand," Grayson said, "Cisco made some threats against her."

"He'd been drinking one night and came to the apartment, but she wouldn't let him in. Cisco got really angry and…" Kathy released a sigh. "He said he'd kill her. I don't think he meant it though. He was just mouthing off."

"How did you feel about it?" Grayson probed, pressing Kathy further. "How did you feel about Melanie's interference?"

"To be honest, I didn't like it either. It seemed like she just wanted to ruin my chances of being happy. Now that I'm older, I can look at the situation differently."

Grayson continued to be relentless with his questioning. "Did it make you mad?"

"Maybe…yeah, a little, but not enough to wish her dead."

"Why did you go along with the restraining order? You didn't have to."

"Because I listened to Melanie. It made sense at the time, but then I started to feel like I'd overreacted."

He kept pushing for answers. "Was there anyone else who

might have been unhappy with Melanie? Could someone have wanted her gone?"

Kathy shook her head and said, "No one comes to mind. Everyone loved her, and she was very popular in school."

Charlie interjected, "Not everyone. It had to be someone who really hated her—someone who would go so far as to murder her."

Kathy's eyes filled with tears. "I wish I could give you more information. I still can't believe what happened. I can't think of anyone capable of such a horrible act."

Grayson retorted sharply, "A moment ago you were thinking of Cisco—is that what you meant by *more information*?"

Kathy stammered in denial, "No! That's not what I meant at all!"

Charlie sighed and put a comforting arm around Kathy's shoulder. "We understand that this is difficult for you, Kathy," she said. "But we need to know everything you can tell us. Even the smallest detail could be crucial in solving this case."

Kathy nodded, wiping away her tears. "I understand," she said. "It's just that I really don't know who could have done something like this. Cisco and Melanie had their issues, but I can't imagine him ever harming her."

Grayson's expression softened. "Okay, Kathy," he said. "Let's move on from Cisco for now. Is there anyone else you can think of who might have had a motive? Was Melanie seeing anyone around the time of her death?"

Kathy thought for a moment, then shook her head. "No, I don't think so," she said. "As for Melanie dating someone… I know she was planning to go to New York a few weeks before she died. She wasn't going alone, but she never told me who she was traveling with—I don't know if it was with a male or a female."

They asked her a few more questions before releasing Kathy, who was now more emotional than before. Grayson noted the darting eye movements, and that her pulse rate had increased—he could tell from the appearance of veins on her neck and throat. The constant licking of her lips indicated her mouth was dry. These were all indicators of lying.

When Charlie escorted Kathy out of the precinct, Grayson leaned back in his chair and let out a deep sigh. He had a strong feeling that there was more to her story than what she had told them. But what could she be lying about? He thought back to the crime scene photos, trying to piece together any clues he may have missed.

"She's hiding something," he muttered when Charlie returned.

"Kathy did really seem nervous about something," she said softly. "And the way she pointed the finger at Cisco but was trying to pretend that she wasn't accusing him." Her voice trailed off for a moment before adding, "She's back on my suspect list."

Grayson nodded in agreement as they made their way to their desks.

"Oh, the next time, don't try to take over *my* interrogation," Charlie stated. "I am the lead on this investigation."

He opened his mouth to defend himself, then thought better of it. Grayson gave a slight nod before walking away.

SIX

Charlie began typing up her notes on the computer. She didn't like feeling as if she'd been played. During the initial investigation, she had taken Kathy off the suspect list because she truly believed in her innocence. Now she was left to wonder why she'd removed her in the first place.

Although it hadn't been planned, she had never seen Grayson in his *bad cop* role while she was the *good cop*. Charlie realized it had forced Kathy out of her comfort zone, shaking her resolve. Still, past experiences had shown her that trusting Grayson would be a mistake. If she wasn't careful, he'd end up receiving the credit for closing the Goins case. Charlie wasn't about to let that happen.

She turned her attention back to Kathy. She was hiding something, and Charlie itched to discover what it could be.

Kathy had known exactly what she was doing when she brought up Cisco Jenner. She wanted to cast suspicion on him without coming straight out and saying it.

Charlie had a feeling that the key to solving the case might be hidden in the tension between Kathy and Cisco. She would have to dig deeper to uncover what it was. Leaning back in her chair, Charlie closed her eyes, trying to piece together the puzzle in her mind.

"I know you're not sitting here napping."

She opened her eyes to find Jen standing in front of her desk, a Cheshire-cat grin on her face. "I was thinking…not sleeping."

"I'm just messing with you, girl."

"Don't you have a robbery crime to solve?" Charlie asked.

"I'm on my lunch break," Jen responded. "I came to see if I could persuade you to join me."

She looked down at her watch. It was almost three thirty. "Rain check, please. I'll run out to the deli across the street and grab a sandwich later. Too much work to do."

"Yeah, you know I don't like that place. I'm going to Mert's…that's my spot."

"I know," Charlie said. "I like to eat there, too, but not every day."

Jen shrugged. "Suit yourself. But don't forget to eat. You're starting to look like you're losing weight."

"I'll grab something later—I promise. I'm working late today."

Jen pursed her lips. "Okay, but I'm holding you to that. Anyway, I'll leave you to it. See you later." She turned on her heel and sauntered out of the department.

With a sigh, Charlie watched her go before returning her attention to the case files on her desk.

It was almost five o'clock when Charlie strolled across the street to pick up her order from the deli.

On the way back to the precinct, she heard someone say, "Charlotte…"

Charlie felt her stomach drop as she came face to face with Samuel Tesarkee, the father who had been absent from her life for so many years. The last time she saw him was at her mother's funeral. She was living with her foster parents at the time, but they thought it was important for her to say a final goodbye. That day, he wouldn't even look at her and disappeared right after the service.

She felt a chill run down her spine, her heart racing. A mix of emotions flooded her mind: sadness, anger and betrayal. She didn't know how he had found her, and she didn't care—she just needed to distance herself from him.

Charlie turned away from him and began walking. She was ready to cross the street, leaving him behind for good, when he reached out to grab her arm.

"Please, Charlotte," he said, his voice full of desperation. "Hear me out. I know I made a lot of mistakes with you, and by leaving all those years ago. But I'm here now and I want to make things right."

Charlie stared into her father's eyes, searching for some hint of remorse in them. But instead of finding it, all she felt was a spark of rage burning inside her. She shook off his grasp and stepped back.

"Make things *right*?" she spat. "Sam, you think you can just waltz back into my life after all this time and everything will be okay? It's not like I missed having a father, because you've never been one to me. I can't miss what I never had."

"I was sick back then, but I'm better now. I've been clean for almost two years."

"I suppose you think I should be happy for you." But Charlie knew it wasn't that simple. She had spent years trying to come to terms with the pain her parents caused her as a child. The constant disappointment, hurt and never feeling safe. "You don't get to come back into my life just because you're sober," she said. "You don't get to erase everything that's happened."

"I know that," he said, his voice low. "But I want to try. Please, just give me a chance."

Charlie looked at him for a long moment, her eyes taking in the man he had become. Sam Tesarkee was older, his face lined with the years that had passed, but there were also crinkles around his eyes that she hadn't seen before, wrinkles that spoke of the way he'd lived his life.

"I'm not doing this with you. Congratulations on being clean and I hope you stay that way. As for me… I'm good and *I don't need you*. Sam, do me a favor and just stay away. We'll both be happier if you do."

"I'm sorry for the way things turned out," he responded. "I hope that you'll be able to forgive me one day."

Charlie met her father's gaze. "It's not likely, but I hope so, too." She reached into her pocket and pulled out a ten-dollar bill.

Sam refused it, saying, "I didn't come here for money. Just to try and make amends. I'm staying at the Lincoln House for men over by Sunrise Christian Church. The church owns the property and runs the program."

Charlie gave a slight nod. "That's good, I guess."

"If you ever want to talk about everything—"

She cut him off by interjecting, "I won't."

Without another glance back, Charlie hurried across the street as soon as the light turned green, leaving behind a ghost of what could have been.

As soon as she entered the building, she was stopped by Grayson.

Charlie glared at him, but inside she was on edge. It was infuriating that Grayson could have this type of effect on her, making her feel things she had worked so hard to bury down deep. Rage bubbled up inside her and she wished she could extinguish the feelings he provoked within her.

"What do you want, Grayson?" Charlie asked, trying her best to keep her voice steady. He should know better than to mess with her when she wasn't in the best of moods.

"I wanted to make sure you're okay. I saw you across the street with that man. The conversation looked heated between you two."

"It wasn't anything."

"Then why are you so upset?" he questioned.

"If you must know…that man was my father, Grayson. As you can see… I'm good. I'm done with this conversation." She held up the bag in her hand. "I'm also on my lunch break."

"Just stop by my desk when you're done."

"Okay," she said before rushing off.

Charlie didn't want him to see the tears that threatened to spill at any moment.

Instead of heading to the break room, she decided to change course and eat her lunch in her car while she got her emotions under wrap.

Grayson had felt a wave of confusion sweep over him when he'd locked eyes with Charlie a few minutes ago. He was taken aback by the burning fire behind them, but there seemed to be a much deeper emotion below the surface. Her lips trembled and her brows furrowed as she desperately held back tears. She'd almost sprinted out of the building.

He felt compelled to see if she was okay and decided to follow her outside. From the parking lot, Grayson watched as Charlie slumped down inside her car and buried her head in her hands, completely overcome by some inner turmoil.

Grayson didn't know anything about her relationship with her father. He'd heard that she had grown up in foster care, but didn't really know whether it was true or not. His grandparents had fostered six children, who they adopted and put through college and the military.

He returned to his desk, but his thoughts were still on Charlie. He didn't like seeing her upset and wanted to reach out as a friend, but she'd never accept his friendship. She had made it quite clear that she didn't trust him.

Charlie was back at her desk thirty minutes later.

Grayson could tell she was still upset, although she was trying to keep her true feelings hidden. He was curious as to what had happened between her and her father but knew better than to pry.

However, by the end of the day, Grayson couldn't help himself. He waited until it was just the two of them in their work area. "Charlie, is there anything I can do to help?" he asked, tentatively.

She looked up at him; her eyes met his. For a moment, he saw a flicker of vulnerability in her gaze, but then it was gone as quickly as it had appeared.

"No. Nothing," she replied, her voice clipped.

But Grayson wasn't convinced. He moved closer to her, his hand reaching out to touch her arm. She stiffened at the touch but didn't pull away.

"Talk to me, Charlie…"

She shrugged in nonchalance. "I'm good. Just had a disagreement with my father. It's nothing important. Anyway, did you need something from me?"

"No," he responded. "I just wanted to let you know that I was finally able to locate Valerie. I left a message for her."

"That's good," Charlie murmured. "Let's hope she calls us back. Cisco is out of town, so I'll check back next week."

"I'll connect with Valerie. I can be pretty persistent," he stated.

Grayson could feel the tension radiating off Charlie, and knew something was deeply troubling her. He wanted to help. She seemed different, completely disoriented and unnerved; it was as if she had been jolted awake from a deep sleep.

"I'll let you get back to work."

"Huh?"

"Nothing," he responded before walking back to his workspace.

A few minutes later, Charlie stood up, packed her tote and headed toward the exit. "I think I'll cut out. I'll see you in the morning."

"Hey, Charlie…you're not alone," Grayson said. "I'm here for you. Whatever you need…"

"I'm good."

"Well, enjoy the rest of your evening," he responded.

"You, too," she stated.

"That was nice of you," Jen said, walking up to his desk. "Charlie's not gonna open up to you until she knows she can trust you."

"At some point there has to be an element of trust between partners."

"True, but does she really see you as her partner?"

"Not at all," Grayson said. "But I'm hoping that things will eventually change between us."

"When her first homicide case was reassigned to you… she really believed that you undermined her. I told her it was all Jamison, but Charlie thinks you had a hand in it as well."

He nodded. "I should've turned it down."

"As if Jamison would've given you the choice…that wasn't gonna happen. Not if you wanted to further your career."

"I hate that it happened," Grayson stated. "Charlie's had it in for me ever since."

Jen gave a short laugh. "I have to be honest. I didn't think you'd last this long."

He chuckled. "I suppose that's fair. I never thought you'd make it in robbery, but I hear you're one of the top detectives in the department."

"I love my job. This is a much better fit for me than homicide was," Jen stated. "I'm about to take my detective exam."

"I'm proud of you," Grayson said with a smile. "You had to overcome a lot, but you did it."

"I know Charlie thinks otherwise, but you really were a good mentor." She checked her watch, then added, "The two of you make a great team. She just doesn't realize it yet."

"You really think so?"

Jen nodded. "I do."

"I saw her earlier today with her father," Grayson announced. "She was really upset after the encounter."

"Oh wow…she hadn't seen that man in years. I'm sure it was a shock to her. Are you sure that she's okay?"

"I asked and Charlie responded she was good. I didn't want to keep pressing her."

"I'll call her when I get home," Jen stated. "How much longer are you planning to work?"

Grayson pushed away from his desk and stood up. "I'll walk out with you. I'm calling it a day. It's been a long one."

SEVEN

Charlie sent up prayers when she left work, hoping to avoid seeing her father lurking somewhere outside the precinct. She hoped that it was abundantly clear to Sam that she had no interest in continuing contact with him. Fear, pain and heartache had been what he'd brought into her life. Now that she was forty, she didn't need or want a father figure anymore.

I don't want to think about this at this moment. Right now, I need to focus on the Goins investigation.

Seeing Sam again left Charlie feeling a mix of emotions. On one hand, she felt proud of herself for having done so well in his absence. But on the other, his sudden reappearance stirred painful memories from her past and reopened the wound her parents had inflicted. She wanted desperately to feel happy, but fear and uncertainty kept getting in the way.

Her phone rang.

"Hey, Jen," she greeted.

"How was your day?"

"I saw Sam."

"How did it go?" Jen asked.

"I told him to stay away from me," Charlie responded. "I don't need a father anymore. And if I did—I'd go to my foster dad before ever reaching out to Sam."

"Was it random? Running into him like that."

Charlie eased down onto the couch in her living room. "Jen, I'm not sure. I walked out of the deli and then I heard someone say 'Charlotte.' I knew it was him as soon as I heard his voice. I had to keep myself from running away. It's like I was a little girl again."

"Do you know where he's living?"

"He's at a ministry home for men," she replied. "I can't think of the name of it right now. His showing up like that has me all messed up."

"Do you want some company?"

"Jen, I'm good."

"No, you're not. I can hear it in your voice."

"I'll be fine," Charlie assured her friend. "I'll make a cup of tea and relax for the rest of the evening."

"I'm a phone call away," Jen said.

"I know and I appreciate you."

They ended the call a short time later.

Charlie made her tea, then settled down with her laptop.

As she leaned back against the plump cushions of her couch, Charlie thought of the countless hours she had spent working on the Goins case. With all of her cases, she became obsessed with finding the suspect, poring over evidence and questioning witnesses—her investigations often took over her life.

She picked up the file and flipped through it once more, her eyes scanning the pages for any new clues she might have missed. And then Charlie saw it—a small detail that she had overlooked before, but now seemed crucial to the case.

Excitedly, she grabbed her phone and dialed Grayson's number. "I think I've found something," Charlie said when he answered. "If you're not busy, would you mind coming over to my place?"

"I just picked up a pizza. Do you mind if I bring it with me? It's enough to share, if you haven't eaten."

She thought about the sandwich she'd discarded in the trash earlier and realized that she was hungry. "What kind is it?"

"Sausage and pepperoni with mushrooms," Grayson responded. "I'll see you shortly."

When he arrived, Charlie liked that he hadn't seemed to notice her loose sweatpants and T-shirt. She was at home and comfortable, not trying to look like a fashion model or impress him. Grayson was focused on what was truly important: finding justice for Melanie. Half an hour later, he and Charlie sat on opposite sides of her dining room table with full bellies, poring over the evidence together, and piecing together the puzzle that had seemed so impossible when she was first handed the case.

"A soror reported that Melanie's phone pocket-dialed her that night—it was before the murder. According to the time stamp, it must have happened shortly after she and Kathy returned to the apartment. It may have some bearing on the case."

"Were you able to hear anything?" he asked.

"It was muffled…inaudible," Charlie said. "Like Melanie was in one room and her phone in another. But you can hear a male and female talking. When I discussed this with Jamison, he said it had minimal evidentiary value."

"Have you considered hiring an audio expert?" he asked. "I know someone who specialized in enhancing a recording like this. I can give him a call if you'd like."

"Sure," Charlie responded. "I'd like to hear the conversation. It might help us in some way. Then again, it might turn out to be nothing."

"There's only one way to know for sure," Grayson responded.

She nodded in agreement, then said, "Jamison tried to reassign this case to someone else, but Chief wouldn't let him. Melanie's parents didn't trust that they'd be kept in the loop. I'd built a rapport with them. When Jamison was fired… I wanted to celebrate."

"I felt the same way," he stated with a grin. "He was a terrible supervisor and nothing more than a bully. I didn't like the way he treated you."

Charlie shrugged in nonchalance. "I'm still here."

"Yes, you are…"

Pulling out his phone, Grayson said, "I'll make the call to my friend."

Charlie knew that by bringing in an expert, they might possibly get some answers. Taking a deep breath, she nodded. "Let's give it a try. It might turn out to be nothing, but at least we'll know."

He smiled before dialing the number for his contact in audio engineering.

Grayson hung up a few minutes later and announced, "Taj is willing to analyze the recording as soon as possible—I just texted you his email address."

Charlie let out a sigh of relief and said, "Thank you so much for this. I really appreciate it."

"We're partners."

Pointing to the pizza box, Charlie said, "And thanks for dinner."

She sent the recording to Taj, then leaned back on the couch feeling a measure of relief. The case had been weighing on her. Charlie considered the chance to finally hear the recording a small victory.

"I just hope your friend finds something useful," Charlie said, biting her lip in anticipation.

Grayson nodded. "Me, too. But even if we don't, we'll just keep digging."

Charlie eyed him, wanting to believe that he was just being a supportive partner. He wanted her to see him differently from the person he used to be, but it wasn't so easy. She thought of Sam, who also wanted her to view him as changed.

She was wary of them both. Charlie hoped to never run into her father again. As for Grayson, she didn't want to work another case with him after this. He was a skilled detective, but she didn't want to spend so much time with him.

"Earlier when I approached you…it was out of concern. I wasn't being nosy," Grayson said.

"I believe you," Charlie responded. "It's just not something I want to discuss. It's too personal."

"I respect that," Grayson said as he pushed away from the table. "It's getting late."

"Thanks again for coming over." She walked him to the door.

"Please let there be something on audio we can use," Charlie whispered as she returned the files to her tote before turning in for the night.

That night, she tried to evict Grayson from her mind.

Charlie decided that it was because they had been forced to work so closely together. She sat up in bed, holding a pillow close to her chest.

"I don't know if I can do this—work with a man I just don't trust."

Charlie was in better spirits by the next afternoon. Her day began with a confession in the Hendrix case. The suspects had been arrested and were being booked downstairs. She felt a sense of accomplishment.

It thrilled her to welcome Phillipa back from her honeymoon with the news that DeShaun Hendrix's case was now closed.

She smiled when Jen stopped by her desk to say, "Congratulations on closing your case."

"Thank you. This is my first with CCU."

"You will have many more, I'm sure. I know how much this means to you."

"Now I can give the Melanie Goins case my full attention," Charlie stated.

"Tonight, we should do something special to celebrate," Jen said. "Let me take you out to dinner. I'll even let you pick the restaurant."

"I'm not choosing Mert's," she responded with a chuckle. "I love their food but I'm in the mood for Italian. I'd like to try that new restaurant on Brookdale Drive."

"Oh yeah… I keep forgetting about that place. We should definitely go there. I'll call to see if we'll need reservations when I get back to my desk."

"If so, can you make it for seven thirty? I'll most likely be here until five-thirtyish."

Jen nodded. "I'll text you."

Smiling, Charlie watched as her friend paused to speak with Grayson before moving on. He had also been Jen's mentor when she worked in the homicide division and they had formed a friendship. Charlie had never allowed her personal feelings toward him to interfere in Jen's relationship with Grayson.

He glanced in her direction. The smile he awarded her was warm, friendly and genuine.

Charlie shocked herself when she returned it with one of her own.

She focused her attention to the closing paperwork for the Hendrix case. Charlie still had eight other active cases outside of Melanie Goins on her desk, but she was either waiting on reports, or still attempting contact with witnesses, officers and detectives on record. The more senior detectives in the unit carried between fifteen and twenty active case files on their desks.

Charlie was grateful for the manageable workload. It allowed her to be more thorough and detail oriented in her investigations. As she filled out the last of the paperwork, her mind kept wandering back to Grayson.

She had always been so focused on her work, not letting anything get in the way of justice. But there was something about Grayson Leigh that made her heart race and her palms sweat.

Charlie shook her head, trying to clear her thoughts. She couldn't let herself get distracted or believe that a man like Grayson could see her as someone other than a coworker. She remembered his ex-girlfriend Lacey, who'd left law enforcement to become a journalist. She was stunning and always looked like she should be on the cover of a fashion magazine. At one point, Charlie assumed Grayson would marry Lacey. She didn't know what happened, but the relationship ended.

She'd heard that Lacey was engaged to be married. Charlie wondered how Grayson felt about the engagement, but she would never bring it up to him. She valued her privacy and respected his as well.

As she sat there lost in thought, she didn't realize that Grayson had walked up to her until he cleared his throat.

"Hey, Charlie," he said with a grin. "Congratulations."

She felt her heartbeat quicken as she looked up at him. He was standing close enough that his cologne filled her senses.

"Just working on some reports," Charlie answered.

"Do you have any recent contact information for Tobias Jacobs? I haven't been able to find anything. He doesn't seem to be on social media either."

"All I have is old information," she responded. "It's possible that he's left town and doesn't want to be found for some reason."

"This makes me wonder why."

Charlie nodded. "I considered that he could be running from something or someone. He acted as if he was afraid, but I couldn't get him to tell me anything. I looked into his background—no red flags. I'll reach out to the university and see if they can tell me anything about Mr. Jacobs."

Grayson checked his watch.

"I've got to attend a mandatory training, so I'll be away from my desk the rest of the afternoon. Text me if anything comes up on the Goins case."

"Have fun," she responded.

Charlie was secretly relieved that Grayson wouldn't be in her line of vision. She would use this opportunity to regroup.

Her eyes scanned the computer screen, tracing line after line of text. The clock on her desk ticked loudly in the background as she tapped her pencil against the wooden tabletop. After an hour of searching, Charlie pushed back from her desk with a sigh. Tobias Jacobs had dropped out in his last year, leaving no forwarding address. She wondered if he had passed away and searched for a death certificate but found nothing.

Charlie leaned back in her chair, rubbing her tired eyes. She couldn't shake off the feeling that something was off, that Tobias's disappearance was not a mere act of dropping out of school.

She stared at the computer screen once more, determined to find something.

Charlie continued scrolling down through the search results until a name caught her eye.

Sarah Jacobs.

She clicked on the link and read the news article.

When Grayson returned, she gestured for him to come over.

"I haven't found Tobias, but I did find his sister," Charlie stated. "Sarah was his younger sister. She was killed in a shooting fifteen years ago. They never found the shooter. The case is cold. I think this is why Tobias wants nothing to do with the police. He has no faith in us."

"It's plausible," he responded. "Was it local?"

"He's from Atlanta," Charlie said. "I couldn't find a driver's license or anything on him. I even checked to see if he was deceased."

"Did you locate any other family members?" Grayson asked.

"That's next on my list," she responded. "Why don't you try to contact Alfonso Levy. Maybe you'll have better luck. If not, move on to Cisco. We can always circle back to him." Charlie picked up her water bottle and took a sip. "I'm going to see if I can make contact with Spring Whitefeather."

Grayson went to his desk and sat down.

She watched him for a moment before picking up the telephone. Charlie wanted to stay on top of who was doing what. She wasn't going to let Grayson get the upper hand in this investigation.

That evening, Grayson left Bible Study shortly after eight o'clock and went straight home, his head swimming with the day's events, including the arrests of the people involved in Hendrix's death.

Tired from a long day, he unlocked the door to his home and flicked on the kitchen light. He pulled a chef's salad out of the refrigerator, cradling it as he made his way to the dining room table.

Grayson took a bite of the lettuce and carrots, but couldn't focus on the food. His thoughts kept traveling back to their recent interview with Kathy—the forgetfulness, her relationship with Melanie, the illness story, the former neighbor's statement…it all seemed vague with lots of missing pieces.

He slowly stirred his fork in circles around the plate as he replayed their conversation in his mind, hoping to fill in some of the blanks concerning that night.

By the time he'd finished eating, Grayson knew he had to talk to Charlie about it, and he knew what he wanted to do next: another interview with Kathy. But he also wanted to talk to Tobias Jacobs and Alfonso Levy. He was especially curious as to why Tobias had been a reluctant witness. Grayson wanted to retrace every inch of Charlie's initial investigation. It wasn't that he thought she'd missed something—it was how he usually worked his own cases.

Grayson spent the rest of his evening checking reports of homicides that took place around the time of Melanie's death. He was looking to see if there were any possible connections. He extended his search to nearby towns.

He knew from Charlie's notes that she'd also reviewed similar crime incidents in the geographic area during her initial investigation. It warranted a second look because bodies could've turned up years later.

Grayson was happy that Charlie had been able to solve the Hendrix murder. He knew it was important for her to close her first case with CCU. He liked seeing her smile—she didn't do it nearly enough. Although Grayson didn't know much about her background, there were subtle clues in her behavior that led him to believe she hadn't grown up in the best of situations. Mostly, it was her inability to trust people. The truth was that he hadn't either, which had been why he would overcompensate for what he viewed as shortcomings. However, he'd started to believe his own lies of self-importance.

As he'd healed from his injuries, Grayson was forced to confront the reality of who he was, flaws and all. He examined the root causes of his issues and wasn't pleased with this self-image, so he prayed for God to help him change into the person He had intended him to be. Grayson still thought of himself as a work in progress, but he was better than he was before.

He readied for bed shortly after midnight. Although he was tired, his mind was still on the investigation. Grayson hoped to get Kathy back to the precinct to probe further. Recalling how upset she got when he questioned her, there was a chance that she might refuse, but it wouldn't be in her best interest. She could also get an attorney involved at this point. He didn't quite know what to expect from her. Right now, things weren't looking too great for Kathy. They were going to keep her on their suspect list until she decided to be forthcoming with everything she knew about Melanie's murder.

EIGHT

Charlie wiped the perspiration from her face, then draped her towel over the handlebar of the bike in cycling class. She had just finished another grueling session, but this time she felt more drained than usual. Charlie looked up at the clock and realized that she had gone beyond her usual time limit for the class.

During her workout, she replayed the interviews with Kathy and Tabitha repeatedly in her mind. She had been so lost in her thoughts that she hadn't noticed the extra half hour that had passed.

As she walked out of the gym, she still felt a little out of sorts. Ever since the sudden appearance of her father, Charlie had been struggling with her inner demons. Exercising had always been a temporary escape for her. But today, even that didn't seem to help.

On the way to her SUV, the morning breeze caressed her face, but Charlie barely felt it. Her mind was preoccupied with thoughts of Sam Tesarkee. She couldn't believe that he had suddenly shown up after all these years.

She stopped long enough to get a smoothie before heading home. This was going to be her breakfast. Charlie watched the server behind the counter as he blended her mix of fruit, protein powder and ice.

She sampled the smoothie as walked into her house. The first taste was sweet and tangy, the ice bathing her tongue in a cool sensation. The fruit flavor lingered on her taste buds: sweet, but not too sweet.

Perfect.

She finished her drink before rushing up the stairs to the shower.

Charlie turned on the water, letting it run hot over her tired body. She took a deep breath and closed her eyes, as steam filled the room. As she lathered up with her favorite body wash, she thought about her agenda for the day.

After she got out, she slipped on a pair of khaki pants, pairing them with a black top and loafers. Charlie ran her hand through her slightly damp hair, fluffing it with her fingers.

She grabbed her tote and went downstairs. It was time to head out to work.

Charlie found herself struggling to keep her focus on the case at hand. Even though Grayson hadn't done anything, a part of her still couldn't help but be wary of him. Despite his reassurances that he wasn't trying to sabotage her again, she couldn't help but feel that it was too good to be true.

Grayson wanted this case solved as much as Charlie did, but could she ever truly trust him? A voice in the back of her mind warned Charlie not to get too close, yet another one yearned for her to put her faith in him. They were partners—an element of trust should exist between them. She trusted him to have her back, but not when it came to the investigation. He'd been honest about being a changed man. She could clearly see that Grayson was not the man he used to be. Charlie still wondered what had caused his transformation. Was it only because of the accident? Or was it something more personal?

But as quickly as those thoughts flooded her mind, Charlie pushed them aside, resolute in her determination to focus on the case.

Grayson was surprised when Charlie walked over to his desk and asked, "Do you have any plans for lunch?"

"I don't, actually." He didn't want to read too much into her question, but hope welled within that she was asking him to have lunch with her.

"Great," Charlie responded. "I was thinking we could celebrate closing the Hendrix case with lunch at Angeline's."

"Sounds good to me," he said, while keeping his expression blank. He didn't want to come off as overenthusiastic for fear it would turn her off.

They left the precinct thirty minutes later.

During the drive, Charlie said, "This is the place I come to whenever I close a case. I consider it a little treat."

Grayson was touched that she'd invited him along. He hadn't expected her to do something like this. He knew that she still didn't trust him.

"I couldn't have done it without you, so thanks for all your help," she said.

"You don't have to thank me, Charlie. We're all a team in the CCU. Phillipa isn't anything like Jamison. She believes a win for one is a win for the entire team. So do I."

"Back then, it was hard to trust you but I took a chance. You betrayed me."

"I know," Grayson interjected. "Only, it wasn't my intent. I gave the man an honest review of your work and he used it against you. Charlie, I'm sorry about that."

"We can't undo the past," she responded.

"You're a great investigator, Charlie. You have to know that."

She seemed surprised by his words.

"I mean it. This is why Phillipa thought we'd make a great team. I believe it, too."

She looked at him. "It hasn't been bad…working with you."

"Never thought I'd hear those words coming out of your mouth."

"To be completely honest… I never thought I'd ever say anything nice to you or about you."

They laughed.

After parking, they walked into the restaurant.

They were seated quickly.

Grayson pretended to study the menu intently while watching Charlie look around the restaurant, taking in the ambience. It was a dimly lit, upscale Italian restaurant. The walls were adorned with vintage Italian posters, and soft jazz music played in the background. She looked back at Grayson and asked, "Have you been here before?"

"Only once and it was a long time ago," he responded. "I came here once with Lacey."

"I suppose you've heard about her engagement."

"I ran into her the week of Phillipa and Kyle's wedding. She told me." Grayson shrugged, then said, "I'm happy for her."

"Are you just saying that to be polite or do you really mean it?"

He eyed Charlie. "I mean it. Lacey deserves to be happy."

"I always thought you'd end up marrying her. She seemed perfect for you."

"Lacey was a friend, one of my closest friends in fact, but it turned out that I didn't love her the way she needed to be loved. Instead of being supportive and loving to each other, we competed with one another over who had achieved what. It was like a game—who would get there first, who would accomplish the most? We both lost out in the process because all the competition just caused tension between us. How were we supposed to listen to each other and support each other when all we could do was compete against each other?"

He read the surprise in her eyes. "Marriage is a huge step and I only want to do it once, so I intend to make sure she's the right woman for me. Right now, I'm taking this time to really work on me. A good woman deserves the *right* man. Don't you agree?"

"That's not something I've ever considered," she responded. "Marriage."

Grayson leaned back in his chair, studying Charlie's face with interest. He had always found her intriguing, and her sudden confession only added to his curiosity. "Care to share why?" he asked, his tone casual.

Charlie shrugged, her expression guarded. "I just don't see the point," she said. "Marriage is just a piece of paper, right? It doesn't guarantee anything."

"But isn't love worth celebrating?" Grayson countered. "Wouldn't you want to share that with someone special?"

Charlie shook her head. "Love is overrated," she replied. "It's just a chemical reaction in the brain. And it never lasts. Just about everyone I know is divorced or unhappy in their marriages."

Grayson couldn't help but feel a twinge of sadness at her words. He had always been a hopeless romantic, and the idea of never finding someone to love was a bleak one indeed. "But don't you want to share your life with someone?" he asked, his voice soft.

Charlie's eyes flickered over to Grayson's face, and for a moment, she seemed to be considering his question. But then she shook her head again, her expression hardening.

"No," she said firmly. "I'm perfectly happy on my own. I don't need anyone else to make me complete."

Grayson couldn't help but feel a little disappointed by Charlie's answer. Although he'd never considered anything romantic in the past, lately he viewed her in a different light. There was a connection; he felt it whenever they were together. Like now.

"Do you know what you're going to order?" she asked.

He hadn't paid much attention to the menu. Scanning it, Grayson said, "Not yet. Everything sounds delicious. When I came before, I had the braised oxtail lumaconi. What do you recommend?"

"You can't go wrong with the spinach and crab ravioli," Charlie responded. "It's delicious but not available for lunch. The chicken *sugo* is also delicious. And of course there's the spaghetti."

"I guess I'll give the spaghetti a try."

Smiling, she said, "I'm getting the chicken *sugo*."

Grayson watched her sitting there before him, her eyes flashing with an intensity that he found both alluring and frustrating, and he felt a stirring within him.

The server came to take their orders.

He ordered the spaghetti, as Charlie had suggested, but his mind was preoccupied with thoughts of the woman sitting across from him. He couldn't help but notice the way her lips curved into a smile as she spoke.

As they waited for their food to arrive, Grayson found himself growing more and more drawn to Charlie. He couldn't explain why, but something about her was captivating. Maybe it was the hints of vulnerability he saw in her eyes.

"What do you like to do for fun?" he asked.

Charlie seemed to consider his question for a moment before saying, "I work out, try different restaurants and enjoy a movie from time to time. What about you?"

"I love to travel," Grayson responded. "I haven't done any since the accident, but I'm looking forward to getting back on the road."

"I've always wanted to see the world," she confessed. "But it's not much fun doing it alone."

"Then invite a friend."

"I have. Jen and I are supposed to take a cruise to Alaska next year."

"That's great. You'll enjoy Alaska."

When their plates arrived, Grayson found himself lost in the taste of the pasta. The sauce was rich and flavorful, and each bite was like a burst of pleasure in his mouth. He stole a glance at Charlie, who was savoring her own plate of chicken *sugo* with closed eyes.

As they both finished their plates, Grayson couldn't help but feel a sense of contentment wash over him. It had been a long time since he had had such a delicious meal, and he was grateful for the experience.

After settling the bill, they headed out of the restaurant.

Grayson turned to Charlie and said, "Thank you for lunch. I had a wonderful time."

She smiled and replied, "I did, too."

"I think we should run a background investigation on Kathy," Grayson announced the moment they returned to the precinct. "I want to know everything about her before we bring her in a second time. Her employment history, credit history…everything."

"Do you think that's really necessary?" Charlie asked.

Grayson wore a serious expression on his face. "Actually, I do. We have to find a way to force the truth out of her."

"I admit that I'm suspicious of her, too," she said. "But

we need to proceed cautiously. We mustn't scare her off—we want her to keep talking."

"I agree."

"To make sure we're on the same page…the reason you want to check Kathy's background is because we're officially considering her as a suspect."

"Yeah," Grayson responded. "Right now, she's at the top of my list."

She gave a slight nod. "Okay. Let's do it."

"Cisco Jenner is back in town and willing to speak with us," Grayson announced an hour later. "But he doesn't want to do it at the precinct. He's fine with us coming to his office."

"Really?"

He nodded. "He owns a gym. The one on Maple. He's expecting us."

"Let's get going then," she responded.

When they arrived, they were greeted by the sound of weights clanking and the smell of sweat as they walked through the gym. Cisco was waiting for them at the reception desk, dressed in a snug-fitting T-shirt that showed off his muscles.

He escorted them to the back of the gym where the offices were located.

"I don't understand why you want to talk to me," he said, closing the door. "There's not a whole lot I can tell you because I don't know what happened that night after Melanie and Kathy left the club."

"I'd like to know more about your relationship with the two women," Charlie stated.

"Melanie was the reason Kathy and I broke up," Cisco responded. "She convinced Kat that I was going to abuse her. That wasn't true. Sure, I got angry but I never laid a hand on her."

"Did you ever threaten Melanie?" Charlie asked.

"Yeah, but I was angry and I just said what I was feeling at that time." Cisco looked from Grayson to Charlie. "Look, I have an anger problem and I might tear up a house, but that's because I don't wanna hit a woman. I'm telling the truth when I say I didn't have anything to do with Melanie's murder. That wasn't me. Y'all know that I was with a date at the club. I spent the night at her place."

"Can you think of anyone who might have wanted to do harm to Melanie?"

"I'm not accusing her of nothing, but I know you want the truth so I'ma give you that. Kat wasn't as close to Melanie as she'd like people to believe," Cisco stated. "Kat felt like Melanie thought she was better than her. She was always talking down to her and treating her like a child. Kat resented that. Just because Melanie was in an abusive relationship, she went around shouting abuse every time people got into arguments. And Kat definitely had a temper on her."

"Melanie was involved with someone abusive?" Charlie asked. This was the first time she was hearing this information. It never came up when she interviewed Cisco after the murder.

He nodded. "That's why she transferred to Charlotte University in the middle of her sophomore year. To get away from him."

"Why didn't you mention this before?" she questioned.

"I wasn't aware you wanted to know about Melanie's past. This happened when she was still living in Virginia."

"Do you know the guy's name?" Grayson inquired.

"I don't know what all the secrecy was about, but Melanie never mentioned his name. I couldn't even get it out of Kat. He played football. That's all I know." Cisco paused a moment, then continued. "Look, I couldn't stand Melanie.

She almost got me kicked out of school over a bunch of lies. After all that stuff happened, I didn't have no time for her or Kat. I wanted nothing to do with them. Kat even tried to get back with me a few times, but I'd already closed that door."

Charlie glanced at Grayson before asking, "What lies?"

"Melanie was going around telling folk that I was abusive to Kat. That was a huge lie."

"You're trying to make us believe you weren't a danger to Kathy," Grayson interjected, "but don't you currently have a domestic violence charge against you?"

Fury lit up his face as he replied, "My baby mama did that. She'd start stuff and call the cops like I was the bad guy. All I ever did was try protecting myself from her. Women know how to hide their—" Cisco paused for a second and seemed to steel himself, before continuing in an even tone, "But that was the old me. Who I used to be. Now I'm different."

"Cisco, can you think of anyone or anything else about that night?" Charlie asked. "Anyone who came into contact with Melanie at the club."

"She talked to a couple dudes…even danced with one of them, but then I wasn't really paying attention to her. My mind was on my date." He paused a moment, then added, "But I did see Melanie and Kat going at it. This was not too long after they arrived."

"They were arguing?" Grayson inquired.

"Yeah. That's when Kat walked off and left Melanie alone at their table. A short time later, they must have made up because I saw them dancing together. Everything seemed cool between them after that."

"You never mentioned this in the previous interview," Charlie said. "Why is that?"

"Because I didn't think nothing of it at the time. People

have arguments all the time and they reconcile their differences. Honestly, I just remembered it."

After they left the gym, Charlie glanced at Grayson. "What's your take on Cisco Jenner?" she asked.

He leaned forward in the passenger seat, resting his elbows on his knees. "I think his version of events is convenient. He's trying to direct the spotlight away from himself and toward Kathy."

Charlie sighed and ran her fingers through her short hair. "Kathy did the same. She slung Cisco into our line of inquiry, but we still need to talk to her again. I want to uncover the identity of Melanie's ex-boyfriend, too."

Grayson nodded in agreement. "Me, too."

They continued discussing Cisco and Kathy all the way back to the precinct.

"I have to say you're right for bringing Kathy in for another interview." Charlie looked up at him, her brown eyes sharp.

"It's necessary. I'm sure that she knows more than she's told us. And then there's her attempt to cast suspicions on Cisco."

Charlie's phone rang, interrupting their conversation. She answered and listened intently before ending the call. "That was the lab. They confirmed that the fingerprint on the wine bottle doesn't match any of the guys on our list. Neither does any of the DNA found under Melanie's nails. They are going to widen the search."

Grayson sat up straight. "I know that's disappointing, but we're going to keep looking, Charlie."

"I know," she responded. "Anyway, let's drive over to speak with Kathy. I want to see what she has to say about this new development."

"Why didn't you want her to come to the precinct?" he asked.

"I feel like she might be more comfortable in her home. I don't want her lawyering up just yet."

Twenty minutes later, they were at her house.

Kathy answered the door, her expression guarded as she looked from Charlie to Grayson. "What are you doing here? I've told you everything I know."

"We just have a few more questions. Do you mind if we come inside?" Charlie asked.

"Sure." She stepped aside to let them enter.

They sat down in her living room.

"We have some new information about that night," Grayson began. "You never mentioned the argument you had with Melanie that night at the club or the fact that she had an abusive ex-boyfriend."

Kathy's eyes widened, and Grayson could see the fear flicker across her face before she quickly regained her composure. "Melanie and I didn't always agree on stuff. It was something minor. As for her ex-boyfriend… I'm sorry, but which one? She dated a couple guys since moving to Charlotte," she replied, her voice barely above a whisper. "I don't know anything about someone abusing her. I know that her father used to beat her mother. That's why Melanie had such strong feelings about everything."

Grayson leaned in closer, his gaze locked on hers. "Are you sure about that, Kathy? Because if there's something you're not telling us, now would be the time to come clean."

Kathy shifted uncomfortably in her seat, her eyes darting around the room. "I swear, I don't know anything."

But Grayson wasn't convinced. There was something in the way she spoke, something in the way her eyes darted from him to Charlie. "We just want the truth."

"I've told you all I know," she responded.

"Kathy, I have a quick question for you," Charlie said. "What did Melanie tell you about her transfer to Charlotte University in the middle of her sophomore year?"

"Melanie told me that she wanted to start over someplace new. She didn't like living in Richmond."

"I have to be up-front with you," Charlie stated. "I don't believe you. We had a conversation with Cisco and he told us that the reason Melanie transferred is because she wanted to get away from her abusive ex-boyfriend. I'm sure Melanie didn't tell him this—it had to be you."

"Have you considered that Cisco is lying to you?" Kathy responded. "He's a good liar."

"Somebody is lying—that's for sure," Grayson said.

"All I know is that she wanted a fresh start after her relationship ended, so she transferred to Charlotte University. She was really upset over her breakup, but she didn't really talk about it. Not with me anyway. Maybe she confided in Spring Whitefeather."

Grayson had Spring on their list, but didn't tell Kathy. They would be speaking to her soon.

"Do you happen to know his name?" Charlie questioned. "The ex-boyfriend."

"Joel Armstrong," Kathy responded.

"The pro football player?" Grayson asked, not bothering to hide his surprise.

"Yes, he's the one."

Charlie seemed just as stunned. "Why didn't you ever mention this before?"

"I don't know," Kathy responded with a shrug. "Since they broke up a long time ago, I guess I didn't think it was important. You really should speak to Spring. I'm pretty sure that she knows more about Melanie's relationship with Joel. Melanie confided in her a lot."

"Did it bother you?"

"Detective Leigh, I don't know why you seem to think that Melanie and I were at odds—we weren't. We did have arguments and disagreements like most people do, but we found ways to resolve them. You should be looking out there for the person who killed my friend instead of harassing me. I've cooperated with you, but if you keep this up—I will get an attorney."

"Do what you feel you must," Grayson responded. "I know that you know more than you're saying. I just don't know why. Is someone threatening you? Because we can protect you, Kathy."

She sneered at his words. "Protect me? From *what*? I don't need protection. And no one is threatening me. I just don't know anything that can help your investigation. Melanie and I were close, but she didn't confide in me about everything happening in her life. I didn't tell her everything about mine."

Charlie sat there, eyeing Kathy closely, as if trying to read her expression.

As far as Grayson could tell, she seemed genuine, but he knew better. He decided to change tactics. "Okay, Kathy. Let's say for a moment that you do know something. Maybe something insignificant that you didn't think was important, but it could actually be a big break in the case. You don't want this person to get away with murdering your friend, do you?"

Kathy looked at Grayson incredulously. "What kind of question is that? You know that I don't."

"Then help us find the person."

She took a deep breath and thought carefully. "I can't give you what I don't have, Detective Leigh. You have no idea how much that night haunts me. I regret leaving Melanie alone.

Maybe if I'd just stayed home…maybe she'd still be alive. My heart breaks a little more each year that passes without an arrest. I watch a lot of crime shows," Kathy stated. "You don't know how many times I've tried to retrace our steps that evening. I want her killer found."

"I want to believe you," Grayson responded. "But my gut tells me that you haven't told us everything."

"When I told you about Cisco—you accused me of trying to point the finger at him."

"We have to consider all options," Charlie interjected. "In our line of work, we see people planting false evidence to throw the police off their trail."

Kathy folded her arms across her chest. "I guess that's your way of saying that I shouldn't take it personally."

Grayson leaned in, his gaze concentrated. "Oh, there's one more question. Were there other knives in the apartment outside the ones in the kitchen?"

"No. Melanie and I split the cost of the set. We wanted knives that wouldn't become dull." She eyed him for a moment before asking, "Are we done?"

"For now," he responded.

NINE

Charlie stifled a yawn as she shifted in her chair later that evening. They had been sitting at their desks for hours, staying late to work on the Goins case. After speaking with Cisco and Kathy, they arranged to meet with Spring Whitefeather the next morning.

She could feel exhaustion washing over her like an incoming tide, but before it fully immersed her, Grayson looked up from the file he was reading and caught her eye. "You look tired."

Charlie forced a smile. "I'm exhausted."

She could feel the weight of his gaze as it lingered on her for a few moments until he returned to his file. The silence in the room was palpable as Charlie tried to focus on the task at hand and keep her mind from drifting toward Grayson, how different he seemed since the accident—softer somehow, yet more intense in his stare.

He suddenly stood up and announced, "I'm going down to get our food. I just got the text."

Charlie nodded.

She watched Grayson walk toward the stairs, her heart in turmoil. Her mind raced with doubts and suspicions. She knew no evidence pointed to any wrongdoing on his part, yet she could not bring herself to completely trust him. Then, running into Sam had brought back a wave of unhappy memories, further complicating her feelings. Her emotions were a tangled mess because of her father and Grayson; they had both brought pain into her life but there was nothing she could do about it. She could stay away from her father, but Grayson was right there every day. Charlie felt a tug of longing inside her as she wondered what it would be like to relax around Grayson, like Jen did. At the same time, she was wary; his easygoing nature could certainly mask something much darker. Would their bond ever reach the depth that the one between Grayson and Jen had?

She didn't want to think about him as anything other than a coworker, but there was something about him that drew her in like a moth to a flame.

Charlie intentionally focused on the file in front of her to keep her mind from wandering.

Grayson returned with their food, breaking her out of her trance. He placed the bag on the table and sat down.

She smiled and thanked him as he handed her the pint-size container of shrimp fried rice. Grayson had ordered the chicken fried rice for himself.

They ate their food, then it was back to the investigation.

Charlie and Grayson had decided to work late to try and formulate a new plan of action.

He strolled up to the whiteboard and posted a photograph of Joel Armstrong. "Let's see exactly how or if he fits in this puzzle."

"He may not really be a person of interest," Charlie said.

"If we can rule him out, that's great, but if not…we move him to our suspect list."

Grayson leaned in closer to the board, his fingers tracing the outline of Joel Armstrong's face. Charlie watched him, fascinated by the intensity in his eyes. He had a reputation for being a little too invested in his work, but in that moment, she found it oddly endearing.

She gave herself a mental shake to stay focused.

It was almost nine thirty when Charlie stood up, saying, "I'm going home. I don't think I can keep my eyes open much longer."

"I need to say something to you before you leave," he said.

She hesitated for a moment before nodding.

They stood in silence.

Finally, Grayson spoke. "I know you have doubts about me, and I understand why. But I want you to know that I would never do anything to hurt you."

Charlie nodded, but the doubts still lingered. "I want to believe you, Grayson. I guess only time will tell."

"Spring, thank you so much for coming in," Charlie said.

"I'm so glad that you decided to reopen the investigation. It's been too long…you know?"

"I do," she responded. "I'm going to put my all into finding Melanie's killer. That's one of the reasons I asked you to come here."

When Grayson joined them in the interview room, Charlie announced, "This is Detective Leigh, my partner. He will be joining us." She still didn't like the idea of a partner, but he was growing on her.

Spring smiled. "It's nice to meet you."

"Same here," he responded.

"It's come to our attention that Melanie transferred to Charlotte University after her breakup with Joel Armstrong."

"Yes, that's true," Spring said. "But surely, you don't think he had anything to do with Melanie's death. Joel loved her. He was a jerk at times but it seemed like he really loved her."

"How do you know this?" Grayson asked.

"Melanie told me. He paid all her fees when she pledged because he knew how much it meant to her. Joel even offered to pay her tuition, but she wouldn't let him. He wanted to be with her—even told her that he'd leave Brittany if she'd just give him another chance."

"Spring, I'm just having a hard time understanding why Joel's name never came up during the first interview," Charlie stated.

"You'd asked me if I knew of anyone who wanted to hurt Melanie," Spring responded. "That wasn't Joel. Besides, she hadn't seen him in a couple years as far as I know."

"We were told that he was abusive."

"His temper used to scare her—that's why Melanie broke up with him."

Charlie laid the pen down on the table. "You seem to know a lot about their relationship."

"That's because Melanie confided in me," Spring responded.

"Tell me about Kathy's relationship with the victim," Grayson said. "Why did she confide in you and not the woman who said they were like sisters?"

"I always thought of them as frenemies. They were fine until they moved in together. That's when Melanie started to see the truth about Kat. She regretted her decision—at least that's what she told me once."

Charlie bit her lip and narrowed her eyes as she asked, "I remember you mentioning this in the initial conversation. Did Melanie ever tell you why she felt that way?" Joel's name had come up so late in the conversation and Charlie didn't have any reason to suspect him yet, but she still felt frustrated by not knowing what was going on. She ran her hands through her short hair and shifted uncomfortably in her seat.

"I think it was mostly because of Cisco. Melanie didn't like him because of his temper...you know."

"Did she tell you that Cisco threatened to kill her?" Grayson inquired.

Spring shook her head no. "Mel didn't tell me anything about that. But I know Cisco and I'm sure he didn't mean it."

Surprised, Charlie glanced over at Grayson before turning back to Spring and asking, "Why do you say that? What makes you think he didn't mean it?"

Spring fidgeted with the hem of her top, her gaze darting between the two detectives. "I just don't think he's capable of something like that. He's a hothead, for sure, but Cisco isn't a killer."

Charlie raised an eyebrow. "You seem pretty sure of that. Have you ever seen his temper in action?"

Spring hesitated before nodding slowly. "Yeah, I've seen it. But he's never gone too far. He's just...intense. You know... He gets worked up and he might kick a door or hit the wall..."

Grayson leaned forward, his expression serious. "So Melanie never talked about feeling threatened by Cisco?"

"No, she just didn't like him because of his temper. She especially didn't like the way he treated Kat."

Charlie tapped her pen against the desk. "Okay, let's move on. What about you, Spring? Did you ever have any problems with Melanie?"

Spring's eyes widened in surprise. "No, of course not. We were friends."

Charlie said, "We're just trying to cover all our bases."

"I understand," Spring said softly. "I just... I don't know how any of this could have happened. Melanie was a good person. She didn't deserve this."

Grayson nodded sympathetically. "We're going to do everything we can to find out who did this, Spring. But we need your help. Is there anything else you can think of that might be relevant?"

Spring shook her head. "No, I don't think so. I'm sorry. But wait…" she said suddenly. "There was something. I didn't mention it before because I forgot about it."

Grayson leaned forward. "What was it?"

"I don't know if this is important, but Melanie met a guy at some bar. She never told me his name, only that he was nice-looking and really interesting, but then a few weeks before she died, she didn't mention him anymore. They were supposed to be going away together, but something happened. I figured things just didn't work out."

"Are you sure she never mentioned his name?" Charlie asked.

Spring shook her head. "She didn't. I'm sorry. I told you about Tobias because he was the most recent person she went out with."

Charlie rose up from the table. "If you think of anything else, please give me a call."

"I will."

She escorted Spring to the exit doors while Grayson went to his desk.

Charlie returned and stopped to talk. "Tobias is still somewhere in the wind—I hope to find him, but in the meantime, I still want to have a conversation with Joel."

Nodding, Grayson said, "Me, too."

"I have a meeting with Phillipa in a few minutes. When I'm done, let's go back over the crime scene photos and reports."

"I have lunch plans but I should be back by two. Can we meet then?"

"Sure," she responded. Charlie wondered if he was involved with someone.

That's none of my business.

A thread of jealousy snaked down her spine at the idea of Grayson dating. She couldn't understand it. Charlie chalked it up to the fact that they worked so well together. Outside of Jen, she hadn't spent as much time with anyone.

Throughout the meeting with Phillipa, she struggled to focus on the task at hand. Her mind kept wandering, and she found herself daydreaming about Grayson. Charlie shook her head, trying to snap out of it. This was not the time for distractions.

Forty-five minutes later, Charlie headed back to her desk. She stole a peek over at Grayson's desk. It was empty. Had he already left?

She felt a pang of disappointment.

Charlie needed to take a break.

She stepped out of the precinct minutes later, letting the heavy door swing shut behind her. She took a deep breath of fresh air and stopped short when she saw Sam standing in front of the deli across the street.

He waved sheepishly when their eyes met.

Charlie stood with her arms folded across her chest as she watched him walk toward her.

"Are you stalking me?"

Sam pushed his glasses up with one finger and shrugged. "No, I was over at the deli," he said. "I'm waiting on my ride home. And I confess that I was hoping to see you, Charlotte."

She cocked an eyebrow suspiciously. "Why? What are you hoping to gain?"

"A relationship with my daughter. On your terms, of course."

Charlie gave a shake of her head. "I don't know, Sam. I just don't think it's a good idea. We have a complicated past, and it's not like we can just sweep it under the rug and start fresh."

Sam's expression softened, and he took a tentative step closer to her. "I know it won't be easy, but don't you want to try? I've missed you, Charlotte. And I know I messed up before, but I'm willing to do whatever it takes to make it right."

Charlie felt her resolve waver as she looked into Sam's pleading eyes.

Sam must have sensed her hesitation because he said, "Please, Charlotte…let me prove to you that I've changed."

"I need to get back to work," she responded. "I'm working on something that requires all of my focus right now." Charlie paused a moment before adding, "Sam, the truth is that I just can't do this with you."

"All I'm asking is that you get to know me and let me get to know you. Get reacquainted."

"I have to think about it," Charlie said. "But do me a favor and stop hanging around the precinct."

"I like the sandwiches they serve at the deli."

"I can't make any promises, Sam. You destroyed any faith I had in you a long time ago. I don't know if I can ever forgive you."

"It's my prayer that one day we will reunite as father and daughter. However, until then, I understand if you need space and time. Just know that I'll always be here for you, Charlotte."

A car pulled up in front of them.

"That's my ride."

Charlie watched him leave with mixed emotions.

There was a time when she yearned for a relationship with her parents, but she couldn't forget the pain they had caused her.

She took a deep breath and tried to push the thoughts out of her mind, returning to the investigation.

However, as Charlie settled back into her workspace, she found it difficult to focus. Her thoughts kept wandering back to Sam and the possibility of reconciliation. She couldn't ignore the feelings stirring within her.

She didn't need any more distractions.

Charlie sat at her desk, staring at the painting on the wall. The details of the Goins crime scene kept playing in her mind on a loop. Eleven years later, the violence of the act was still unsettling to her, and the fact that the killer was still out there added to her anxiety. She didn't like that a killer was roaming free because she hadn't caught up.

Charlie picked up the autopsy report once again and read through it. Melanie had fought hard, but the killer had been relentless. The image of the twenty-two stab wounds on the victim's body made her feel sick to her stomach. She wondered what kind of monster could do something like this.

When Grayson returned from lunch, they would retrace Melanie's steps with a focus on the evidence, more specifically the missing knife. The only thing they knew about the weapon was that it was a fixed blade knife. She recalled a case Grayson caught right before he transferred to the CCU, involving a knife.

It had been a brutal murder, with the victim's body left in a pool of blood on the living room floor. Grayson had been the lead detective on the case and she remembered the way he'd described the crime scene and the way a knife had been plunged into the victim's chest repeatedly, until he bled out. They had found the knife nearby, covered in blood and fingerprints. Grayson had spent weeks gathering evidence and building a case against the suspect, eventually securing a conviction and putting the killer behind bars.

But now, as Charlie sat there with Melanie Goins's case in front of her, she kept wondering what they were missing. The autopsy report showed that she had been stabbed in the abdomen, chest, neck, and chin; she'd also sustained facial injuries. Melanie's death was due to the laceration of the left ventricle of the heart and to the hemorrhagic shock produced by the multiple wounds.

Jen walked over saying, "Want to grab some lunch?"

"Not today," Charlie responded. "I need to talk to Grayson about a case. Another time?"

"Sure. I'm going to Randy's Deli. Do you want me to bring you something back?"

She was surprised Jen wasn't going to her usual place, but didn't comment on it. "I'm good. Thanks."

Charlie sat there for a few more moments, staring at the report. The wounds seemed too precise, too calculated. She knew it wasn't just a random attack. It was planned. Someone had wanted to hurt Melanie, to inflict as much pain as possible before finally killing her.

Grayson walked through the department doors, laughing and talking with another detective. Her heart leaped with joy when she discovered that he'd had lunch with Lou Dobbs, although it shouldn't have mattered to her. She gave him a few minutes to settle down before picking up the file and walking to his workspace.

TEN

Grayson noticed a figure approaching his desk. It was Charlie. She sat down and immediately started talking. "I just went back over the crime scene photos." She handed them to him.

The sight of Melanie's lifeless body, riddled with stab wounds, made Grayson's stomach churn. He couldn't imagine the pain and fear the victim must have felt in her last moments.

"I was just thinking about that case you investigated…" Charlie said. "It was the last one you worked before leaving Homicide."

"Oh, the Hernandez case," Grayson responded. "That was definitely rage. He was messing around with the wrong woman."

"I know you did extensive research on knives back then. The knife used to kill Melanie was a fixed blade like the one used in that murder."

"The one in the Hernandez murder was a Becker knife by Ka-Bar," he said.

"I remember the reporters calling it a *Rambo* knife."

Grayson chuckled. "I initially thought it was a USMC fighting knife until we found the weapon in the suspect's closet."

"Regarding the Goins case," Charlie said, "What we know is that the linear cuts on Melanie's body suggest that a knife with a thick blade had been used. The killer had to bring the knife with them. Which would explain why none of the knives in the apartment matched the murder weapon."

Grayson nodded slowly, considering the idea. If the killer had brought the knife with them, that meant they had planned Melanie's murder in advance.

"Her death was premeditated," Charlie stated. "This wasn't a crime of passion or some argument that escalated."

He agreed.

Holding up a photograph of the note, she said, "'I'm not stupid…' Those words… I've been trying to figure out what it means. The words almost feel like a taunt."

"It's obvious we're dealing with a very angry person," Grayson said after a moment. "For whatever reason, someone really wanted to punish Melanie. It was almost sadistic."

He picked up the photograph of the note that was left near the victim's body and stared at it.

Charlie studied him carefully before asking, "I can tell something's bothering you about that note. What's on your mind?"

"Blood was splattered all over the room, but there isn't any on the note," Grayson said.

"I noticed that the night I did the initial investigation," she responded. "Which suggests that it could've been written away from the crime scene or some time before the murder."

"My observation is that whoever wrote this didn't use their dominant hand…"

"To disguise their handwriting," Charlie finished for him.

"There's something about the way the word *stupid* is written." Grayson passed the photograph to Charlie. "Look at each letter carefully."

"I think I can see what you mean," Charlie said reluctantly, not wanting to admit she hadn't seen it before. She examined each letter, not wanting to miss any clues. The more she studied the note, the more convinced she became that something was off about one of the letters. "The *P* is definitely different from all the other letters. More defined, almost as if it had been purposely written with an extra emphasis." She glanced up at Grayson and saw a knowing gleam in his eye.

"I think the person who wrote the note forgot for a moment that they were trying to disguise their handwriting. Notice the little curl at the bottom—this suggests that our mystery writer is a female."

"So, you're thinking…"

"I'm actually wondering why it was there," Grayson said. "It had to be written beforehand because it doesn't make sense to leave a message like this for Melanie after she's dead. I'm thinking our victim either received the note before she was killed or the killer put it there to lead the investigation down the wrong path."

"I'm not sure that I agree with your theory completely," Charlie responded. "I don't think it was written to mislead us. The tone of the note was angry and Melanie's murder was definitely about rage. My instincts tell me that it's connected in some way to that night."

"According to this report, the victim drank wine shortly before her death," Grayson stated. "The average glass of wine can take three hours to leave a person's system. This wasn't a cheap bottle of wine either."

"Melanie liked wine. Her roommate said she had a glass to help calm her nerves from time to time. She claimed that Melanie didn't drink while at the club—just danced. According to Kathy, she assumed Melanie had gone to bed before she left the apartment that night."

"Maybe that's what the victim wanted her to believe," he suggested. "She could've been expecting company."

Charlie rejected the idea. "I'm not sure she knew that Kathy left for the night. Melanie likely didn't know she was by herself in the apartment until it was too late."

"Then why didn't she call out for help?" Grayson queried.

"Because she recognized the person who did it." Holding up the picture of the wine bottle, Charlie said, "I think it's more probable that she was already incapacitated by the time her attacker entered the apartment."

Grayson raised an eyebrow. "Incapacitated? As in whoever did this to her probably drugged her before they even entered the apartment."

She nodded. "Or it could've been on Melanie's part. She had a prescription for Xanax. It was found in her system along with alcohol. It's possible she drank a couple glasses of wine, then took a pill to wind down for bed. When the killer showed up, Melanie was still able to put up a fight. Maybe he wanted to get intimate, but she refused and things took a violent turn."

Grayson was thoughtful for a moment before nodding in agreement. "It's a plausible theory—certainly one worth considering. We need to find out who had a motive to kill Melanie." His voice was low and intense. "We need to look at everyone in her life at that time, from her family and friends to her coworkers and acquaintances."

"We also need to revisit her past," Charlie said. "See if there were any other incidents or relationships that could have led to this."

The next day, Charlie started her morning off at the gym. She didn't have to go into the precinct today, but it didn't mean that she wouldn't get some work done. After her exercise class, she intended to head home to shower and change before meeting with one of the victim advocates assigned from the district attorney's office to consult on one of her other cases.

After that she went back to her house and spent the afternoon in her office. Charlie reviewed and compared both Kathy's and Spring's interviews from the initial investigation and their most recent ones, as well as the voice stress analyzer reports.

Kathy was now at the top of her suspect list.

Charlie took a sip of coffee and watched closely as the video of Kathy's first interview began. On screen, she sat with her back straight in the chair, her hands folded neatly in her lap as she answered questions. Every now and then, Kathy's gaze shifted slightly in midsentence, or she pursed her lips tight for a fraction of a second before continuing.

As Charlie began to ask more personal questions, Kathy's demeanor changed. Her voice became shaky and her hands trembled slightly as she struggled to answer. Charlie could see the pain etched on her face, and she remembered feeling sympathy for her.

Suddenly, Kathy's mask slipped. She began to sob uncontrollably, her body shaking with each convulsion. Charlie felt her own heart breaking for her as she witnessed her unraveling before her eyes.

There was something she'd missed until now. Kathy looked up at the camera with an expression of utter despair.

She did it on purpose, Charlie realized. Almost as if she were on the set of a movie. Her mind raced as she tried to make sense of what she had just realized. Was Kathy putting on an act for the camera? Or was she genuinely in such emotional distress that she couldn't control herself?

A wave of disappointment washed over Charlie, followed by anger. She'd believed Kathy was innocent despite everything Spring had insinuated back then. Now it was looking like she might have murdered her roommate that night. Their neighbor Tabitha heard what she said were two people arguing and then a thud. It was possible Kathy and Melanie had gotten into a fight, but why?

Charlie considered the note and the fact that it had been written by a woman. Kathy hadn't submitted a handwriting sample because Charlie had never asked her to do so.

I should've covered my bases better.

Her mind was in turmoil, thinking about all the possibilities. Charlie was conflicted over whether Kathy was really capable of killing someone. She couldn't rule out the possibility that maybe someone wanted her to look guilty. But who would go through the trouble to try to frame her? Cisco?

Charlie needed to gather more evidence before jumping to any conclusions. There were still so many unanswered questions about the case, and she was determined to find out the truth. She really wanted to track down the unknown witness who could also be the suspect. It was possible they held all the answers.

Charlie was waiting for him when Grayson pulled into the precinct parking lot the next day. She looked as if she had some new information to share.

"Did something happen?" he asked as soon as he got out of his car.

"Spring called me a few minutes ago. She asked that we come to her boutique."

"Did she say why?"

Charlie shook her head. "I'm assuming she's ready to tell us everything she knows. At least I'm hoping someone will talk."

He gestured to his vehicle. "Get in."

They arrived at the shop twenty minutes later.

Spring let them inside. "I don't open for another hour, so we can talk freely."

Grayson and Charlie followed her to her office.

"I asked y'all to come because I thought about everything you both said. I'm going to tell you everything I know about Joel and Melanie's relationship—everything she told me. But I still don't believe he had anything to do with her death."

"We'd appreciate it," he said.

"Melanie was head over heels in love with him, but Joel's temper scared her. It's why she left Richmond, Virginia, and came to Charlotte. She felt that if she'd stayed in Richmond, things might have gotten worse between them and she didn't want that to happen. From what Melanie told me…she hadn't seen Joel since she changed schools and I believe that to be true," Spring said. "However, I do know that he reached out to her a couple of times."

Eyeing her, Charlie inquired, "Do you remember when?"

"He emailed her about six months before she was killed," Spring responded. "We had just left a friend's party. He wanted to see her. She told me that Joel had emailed her once before when he first started playing with the Charlotte Bears NFL team, but she didn't respond. When we got back to my place, Melanie changed her mind and called him. Joel had sent his number in the email. They ended up arguing though because she refused to let him come over."

"Why did she change her mind about contacting him?" Charlie questioned.

"I think she initially wanted to see Joel. But then the conversation went way left. Melanie hung up on him, but not before telling him that she knew all about some woman he'd been seeing. She said something about it being foul. And that he only did it to hurt her."

"She didn't mention a name?" Charlie asked.

"Not that I could hear. I left the room to give her some privacy."

Charlie scribbled down notes in her notepad, still trying to piece together everything. "Did Melanie ever come straight out and say that Joel was abusive?"

Spring shook her head no. "Melanie grew up watching her stepfather beat her mother. One day her mother pulled a gun on him. That's when she took Melanie and left—they never looked back. Melanie said she'd never tolerate any form of abuse from anyone."

"I'd like to know your honest thoughts on Melanie and Kathy's relationship," Grayson said. "I want straight answers—no sugarcoating."

"Like I told you before—they were frenemies. They didn't really like each other, but since they had to live together, they made the best of their situation." She paused a moment, then said, "Melanie was actually planning to move out when the lease ended. She and I were going to get a place together."

"Why did you stop being roommates in the first place?" he asked.

"I was moving in with my boyfriend." Frowning, she added, "Big mistake."

Grayson mulled over her answer for a moment, trying to piece together the puzzle of these women's lives. He wondered what caused the tension between Melanie and Kathy.

He cleared his throat before asking, "Do you have any idea why they didn't get along?"

Spring hesitated a moment before answering, "Could be personality, but I really think it had to do with some guy they both liked. Melanie wouldn't really tell me anything about it, but I heard part of an argument they had. I overheard her tell Kat that she should've honored the friend code. All I can tell you is that it caused a lot of drama between them."

"You don't have any idea who the guy was?" Charlie asked. She swallowed hard, and he wondered if she was frustrated at hearing this for the first time.

"I don't," Spring responded. "But I don't think the relationship lasted too long after. Kat sulked around for a bit, then eventually she was back to her usual self."

"Are you sure you don't remember Melanie seeing anybody else back then?" Charlie asked.

"Melanie didn't like to talk much about her dates unless she thought they had substance."

When they left the boutique, Charlie said, "I'm thinking the unknown witness is the guy Melanie and Kathy were involved with."

Grayson nodded in agreement. "It's definitely a possibility. The victim was dating this guy—might not have been serious, but then Kathy starts seeing him, too. She and Melanie are at odds because of it."

"It's also possible that this dude wanted to date both women. Maybe this was some fantasy of his," Charlie stated. "Having two women fighting over him."

At the precinct, Grayson went to his desk while she checked in with Phillipa to update her on their progress.

After her meeting ended, she sat down at her desk and made a few phone calls.

Charlie hung up the phone fifteen minutes later and bolted from the chair, her heart racing with a sense of urgency.

She walked briskly over to Grayson's desk. He was staring at something on his computer screen.

Charlie cleared her throat to get his attention and he turned toward her.

"The Bears are playing at home this weekend. Joel Armstrong is at the stadium right now—they're practicing. I think we should head over there to talk to him."

Grayson leaned back in his chair, confusion etched across his face. "I still don't get why he wasn't brought up before."

Curling her fingers into a fist, Charlie uttered, "Apparently Kathy nor Spring thought it was important to tell us that he'd communicated with Melanie before she died. I mean… it might not be anything, but it would've been nice knowing about all this back then. Grayson, I asked pretty much the same questions each time I spoke with them."

"It happens," he responded. "We don't always get everything in the initial interview. Unfortunately, people judge what is and isn't important at times. I checked and the night she was murdered—he wasn't playing football," Grayson stated. "But what we don't know is if he was in town." He slowly stroked his chin in thought before adding, "Joel's fiery temper is legendary."

"He's officially on the suspect list," Charlie said. "Right up there with Kathy and Cisco as far as I'm concerned."

Grayson agreed that they had to consider all possibilities to find the killer.

They prepared to head to the stadium for a conversation with Joel.

"I don't have any idea how this is going to go," Charlie said.

"As long as he tells us the truth—there isn't anything to worry about," he responded. "Unless he confesses to murder."

Charlie chuckled. "I highly doubt that's about to happen. A person can hope though."

They walked out of the precinct, got into a car and were soon on their way.

Upon arrival, Charlie compared the football stadium to a Roman amphitheater where gladiators met the lions, with the exception of the steel beams supporting its structure.

They flashed their badges at the security guard who let them through without a hassle.

Charlie and Grayson sat down and watched as the players in uniform and helmets tackled dummies, ran plays, caught passes and performed other drills while their coaches barked orders at them. The players' muscles merged together, writhing like ropes. They'd catch Joel on the way out of practice and question him.

"Did you ever dream of playing for the NFL?" she asked.

"Yeah, when I was in elementary school," Grayson responded. "But reality set in when I got to high school."

"What happened?"

"A bad knee injury," he said.

"I guess you miss all this," Charlie said. "The smell of sweat, dirt and grass."

"Not really. I still enjoy watching the game, but I don't miss the injuries."

"C'mon, man," one of the coaches yelled. "Let's go…"

After the practice, they made their way to the locker room, where they found Joel putting away his football gear. The sound of a locker slamming shut caused Joel to turn around, surprise written on his face when he saw the detectives.

"Who are you?" Joel asked cautiously.

He stood tall and muscular, his muscles bulging beneath his practice jersey. Dark-skinned, he wore his hair in a military buzz cut.

"Joel Armstrong," Grayson said. "I'm Detective Leigh and this is Detective Tesarkee."

"What can I do for y'all?"

"We came to ask you a few questions about the night of Melanie Goins's murder," Grayson said, his eyes trained on the athlete.

Joel's face paled slightly, and he turned his gaze to Charlie, openly assessing her. "That was a long time ago. Why the sudden interest now?"

"We've reopened the investigation," she stated.

Joel's eyes narrowed. "What are you trying to say?"

"Is there somewhere we can speak in private?" Grayson inquired.

Joel eyed the two detectives warily, but then gestured for them to follow him into an empty office across from the locker room. It was small and cramped, with stacks of papers and playbooks piled high on the desk and shelves lining the walls.

Charlie and Grayson each took a seat in the two armchairs Joel had pushed together in front of the desk.

"So, what is this really about?" Joel asked, leaning back in his chair. "If you think I had anything to do with her death—you've got the wrong person. I'm afraid I don't see how I can help you. We dated for a while in college, then she transferred to Charlotte University."

"We only found out recently that you two were involved," Grayson stated. "We know that you weren't playing football the night she died, and we also know about that temper of yours. We know that Melanie broke up with you because she was afraid of your temper. Maybe she was worried that you'd hit her. Maybe you did lay hands on her."

Joel's face paled. "That's not true," he answered, his voice barely above a whisper. "We had our share of problems, like any other couple."

"We were told it was a little more than that," Charlie said, her eyes never leaving Joel's face. She was bluffing and wanted to gauge his reaction. "Are you going to deny that you got physical with Melanie?" Her words hung in the air like a noose.

A slender woman with ash-blond hair and blue eyes entered the room, saying, "There you are… I've been looking for you."

"This is Brittany…my wife," Joel then introduced them.

"Detectives, why are you here to see my husband?" she asked while taking a seat. "Has something happened?"

He gave her a quick recap. "They're here about my ex-girlfriend Melanie."

"The one that was murdered?" Brittany frowned in confusion. "Why are you talking to him? Their relationship ended a long time ago. He hadn't seen or spoken to her in years. Right, babe?"

He nodded.

Charlie and Grayson exchanged a glance before turning back to Brittany. They both knew he was lying,

"We understand that, ma'am," Grayson said. "However, we have reason to believe that your husband may have information that could help us with the investigation. At best, we'd like to rule him out as a suspect."

Brittany's expression tightened, and she leaned back in her chair. "Did you hear me? Joel has nothing to do with this. He would never hurt anyone."

Charlie remained calm despite the woman's hostility. "We're not accusing him of anything, ma'am. We just need to ask him a few questions."

Joel placed a hand on Brittany's shoulder, offering a reassuring squeeze. "It's okay, honey. I'll talk to them."

Brittany looked at her husband, worry etched on her face. "You don't have to do this."

"I don't have anything to hide," he responded. "I'd rather get this over with now and be done with it."

"Fine, but I'm staying in here with you." She looked over at Grayson. "I'm an attorney."

Unfazed, he nodded.

"Joel, when was the last time you saw Melanie?" Charlie asked.

"I never saw her after she left Richmond. I did reach out to her when I started playing with the Bears. Melanie never responded, so I figured she didn't want to be bothered."

"Is that the only time you contacted her?"

He nodded.

"We have a statement from a witness that says you contacted Melanie at least twice before she died."

"That's a lie," Brittany stated. "Why would he have done something like that after all that time?"

Charlie looked at Joel. "We'd all like the answer to that."

"I did reach out to her," he said, his voice low. "It was like six or eight months before she died. I just wanted to make amends. I didn't like the way we ended things."

"We were living together during that time," Brittany stated.

She looked and sounded surprised; Charlie noted.

"I know," Joel responded. "Mel and I didn't even talk that long. I apologized and wished her well. That was about it."

"Why didn't you ever mention it?" his wife questioned.

"Would you be willing to give us a DNA sample?" Charlie interjected.

"No." Brittany objected before Joel could respond.

"Is there a problem?" Grayson asked, raising an eyebrow.

"I just don't see why Joel needs to give a DNA sample," she said, her voice wavering slightly.

"Standard procedure," Charlie said with a shrug. "We need to rule out everyone as a suspect."

Joel looked at Brittany, his eyes filled with an unspoken question. She shook her head slightly, and he turned back to Charlie. "I'm sorry."

Brittany spoke up, "We have nothing to hide, but we must protect our privacy. I'm sure you understand."

Charlie could feel her blood boiling at Brittany's response. She had been a detective for years and had seen her fair share of suspects try to avoid giving DNA samples. Usually, it meant they had something to hide. His wife's sudden intervention only added to her suspicions.

Grayson, on the other hand, had a different approach. He was known for using charm to get his way. "Ma'am, we understand your concerns, but it would really help us in our investigation if we could get a sample from your husband. We promise to keep his privacy in mind and only use it for this case."

Brittany looked at Grayson, considering his words before standing up. "It's time we get going," she announced. "Joel and I have to meet with his agent."

Charlie had a strong feeling that he would've complied with their request had it not been for his wife's objection.

She and Grayson made their way out of the stadium, the sun hitting their faces as they walked into the parking lot.

Charlie looked over at him and glimpsed a sense of longing in his eyes as Grayson looked back at the stadium.

"You do miss it, don't you?" Charlie said with a grin on her face.

He laughed it off but she could see right through him.

For a moment, the two of them were silent until Grayson finally spoke up.

"I miss playing at times," Grayson confessed, looking at Charlie.

Charlie nodded her head, taking a deep breath in.

"I didn't have the best of childhoods. Sports was my escape from my life—a temporary outlet. On the field… I could be whoever I wanted to be."

"That's good that you had something like that," she responded.

"Yeah. I had a couple coaches who became like mentors. They believed in me and encouraged me to do my best. One of them was a deputy sheriff. He's the reason I'm in law enforcement today." Grayson paused a moment, then continued. "After the accident, I had to have physical therapy and it was a struggle for me. They had to replace my left knee. All I could think about was that I'd never be able to play football again. Some of my friends from college and I would still get together to toss the ball around. It's a stress reliever."

"Why can't you play football?"

"Because high-contact sports like that can loosen and wear down my implant."

"That accident took away the one thing you loved most then," Charlie said.

"But I still have my life," Grayson replied. "I'm still here. I didn't realize just how much I wanted to live until I felt myself dying. When I was losing consciousness, I heard this voice say, *fight if you want to live.* I began to pray and ask God for strength to make it through. The pain… I never want to go through anything like that again. In that moment, nothing else mattered. Success…the job…nothing but having the chance to grow old."

"One wouldn't know you'd gone through anything to look at you now," Charlie said. "To be honest, I'm a bit surprised that you're already back at work."

"I got tired of sitting at home doing nothing."

The two of them continued walking until they reached their vehicle.

She glanced over at Grayson. He had almost died, but through his ordeal, he never gave up on God. In fact, he seemed to have gotten closer to Him.

"Did you ever blame God for any of the stuff you had to go through in your life?" Charlie inquired.

"No, not at all. I couldn't blame God for the choices my mother made. She chose to get involved with a married man and have a child with him. Her choices led to her having to work two jobs just to keep a roof over our heads. There wasn't any extra, so there were times when we would have to split one hot dog and a can of beans. She made too much money for food stamps. She was too proud to ask her parents for help, so I wore clothes donated from the church…one of the members would adopt us for Thanksgiving and Christmas. We basically relied on the kindness of strangers, but I kept telling myself that one day things would be different."

"When did they change for you?"

"In middle school. Coaches started to take notice of my athletic abilities. College coaches, too. They started coming to see me play during my freshman year in high school. I had speed, vision…everything they wanted in a wide receiver."

"I heard that you were an NFL draft pick."

Grayson smiled. "I was. An injury during training camp put an end to that dream. So, I became a police officer."

"It had to be hard to give up on your dream."

"Charlie, I had more than one dream. I had other aspirations, such as maybe becoming a lawyer, but decided to go into law enforcement. I truly love what I do."

"I pictured an entirely different life for you."

"That's what I wanted," he responded. "I wanted to be the picture of success…a person who was always winning… I wanted to be the best. But then I realized that none of this impressed God. He didn't care about any of that—He was only concerned with the condition of my heart."

"It's nice to be able to finally meet the real Grayson Leigh," Charlie stated.

"One day I'd like to meet the real Charlie Tesarkee." He unlocked the car door and held it open for her.

She was too stunned to say anything. She sat down on the passenger side looking straight ahead.

"Why do you think Brittany was so quick to stop Joel from giving us a DNA sample?" Grayson asked, breaking the tense silence in the vehicle.

Charlie shrugged. "Maybe she doesn't want us to find something that might incriminate him." She was relieved that he'd changed the subject.

He nodded thoughtfully. "Did you see her expression when Joel admitted that he'd contacted Melanie?"

"That look she gave him was very telling. Brittany Armstrong has a jealous streak. She's definitely not into sharing her man."

Grayson chuckled. "I wouldn't want to be Joel right now. I'm sure she's interrogating him about reaching out to Melanie."

As they continued driving, Charlie felt a sense of satisfaction spreading through her body. This investigation was getting interesting, and she loved a good challenge.

ELEVEN

Grayson and Charlie opened the take-out containers of steaming Chinese food, their hunger temporarily taking precedence over the murder investigation.

She reached for a pair of chopsticks while he opened up the police database and began searching for any other incidents involving Joel Armstrong.

Charlie furrowed her brows and took another bite of her General Tso's chicken.

Grayson watched in silence, noting the crease between her eyebrows. "Okay… What's on your mind, Charlie?" he asked.

"I don't know," she said, wiping her mouth with a napkin. "It just doesn't make sense. Joel Armstrong has no history of domestic violence that I've been able to locate so far. Not even when he was in college. Yet Kathy is under the impression that he hit Melanie. It upset her enough that she left school and came to Charlotte. However, according to Spring, Melanie never outright said that he was abusive toward her. My thoughts are, if it really happened, then there should be a record of this somewhere. I don't believe that Melanie transferred to another school because Joel had a bad temper. Something more had to happen."

He nodded thoughtfully. "Either Melanie didn't report it

or it was wiped under the rug because he was the star football player at the time. What about her mother? Maybe she confided in her."

"I'll give her mother a call." Charlie picked up her phone. Sonya Goins answered right away.

"Hello?"

"Hello, this is Detective Tesarkee," Charlie said. "I'm here with Detective Grayson Leigh. We have you on speaker."

"I hope you're calling with good news," Sonya replied.

"We're still in the middle of this investigation, but I have a couple questions that I believe you can help me with."

"Sure. What is it?"

"It's come to our attention that Melanie was dating Joel Armstrong when she attended the University of Richmond."

"She did," Sonya confirmed. "She changed schools after they broke up. Mel said that he accept the breakup well. We thought it best to put some distance between them. It's a good thing, too. I've read the stories about him and his anger issues. I think my daughter was afraid of Joel."

"Why do you think that?"

"Mel witnessed the abuse I suffered at the hands of her father. She had zero tolerance for men who didn't exhibit control over their tempers. She wanted nothing to do with anyone like that. She told me that they scared her."

"Do you think Joel ever hit Melanie?"

"No," Sonya answered. "She would've told me. I was the one who suggested that she change schools. I didn't want her to walk around campus feeling afraid—I thought it best that Mel start over at a new school. My daughter never would've kept something like that from me."

"Thank you. We'll be in touch if we have any more questions or if there's a development in the case," Charlie said, before she and Sonya said their goodbyes.

"Do you think Melanie lied to Kathy about being in an abusive relationship?" Grayson asked once Charlie was off the phone. "Maybe to get her to see the truth about Cisco."

"It's a possibility," Charlie responded as Grayson cleared away their take-out containers.

As they dug deeper into Joel's personal life, they discovered something buried beneath all the articles written about his impressive athletic career.

"Okay, here we go… Joel Armstrong was arrested three years ago for assaulting a woman in a bar," Charlie announced as she read the police report. "But then the victim suddenly changed her mind and decided not to press charges."

"Payoff…" Grayson said.

Charlie nodded solemnly. "They usually get away with stuff like this if there's money involved. We should pay him another visit when the Bears are back in town to ask him some questions about it. *Without his wife.* I know she's his attorney, but I'd still like to try and talk to him alone."

"You think I can get him to sign my jersey while we're at it?" Grayson asked with a smirk.

Charlie continued to dig deeper into Joel Armstrong's past. She spent hours scouring the internet for any articles or interviews that mentioned him.

As she delved deeper, she found more and more instances where Joel had let his anger get the best of him, stemming all the way back to high school. There were stories of bar brawls, road rage incidents and even a rumor that he had once thrown a chair across a hotel room during a fit of rage.

Charlie found in two of the incidents Joel was ordered to take court-ordered anger management classes. "Doesn't look like it's helping," she mumbled to herself. "This is one angry man."

From all appearances, Joel looked warm and friendly. He didn't appear to be a hothead. Brittany didn't seem to be afraid of him either. His wife didn't cower or back down—in fact, Charlie could've easily assumed that she was the one in charge.

She had seen men like Joel before. Men who appeared to be gentle and kind in public, but behind closed doors, they turned into monsters. Her own father was an example. If Charlie found evidence proving that Joel had turned his ire on Melanie, she wasn't about to let Joel get away with it.

Charlie's search finally led her to a small, obscure article buried deep within the internet. It documented a domestic violence incident that occurred in Joel's apartment complex nearly fourteen years ago. The victim's name had been redacted, but she wondered if it involved Melanie.

The article detailed how the police had been called to Joel's apartment after reports of a disturbance. When they arrived, they found a woman with a black eye and bruises on her arms. Joel had been arrested and charged with domestic violence. Charlie's heart sank when once again, the victim didn't want to press charges.

She knew that this could be the evidence she needed to prove that Joel was capable of hurting Melanie, and printed out the article.

She wanted to hear Grayson's thoughts on all she'd found.

Charlie sat across from Grayson, staring intently at the information they'd gathered so far. They had been working together for a few weeks now, but there were times when Grayson felt like Charlie was only tolerating him. Once they closed the Goins case—she'd want nothing more to do with him.

He stole a glance at her, admiring the way she scrunched up her face whenever she found something that just didn't feel right. She was beautiful, and Grayson was attracted to her, but he didn't want to risk ruining their working relationship.

Charlie shifted in her seat, breaking Grayson out of his reverie.

"What do you think of my theory about Melanie being the victim in this article?" she asked, looking up at him.

"It's plausible, especially since it's around the time she left the University of Richmond. Makes sense to me. She loved him and that's why she didn't press charges, so she did the next best thing—she moved away to get away from Joel."

"Do you think we're making any progress?"

Grayson cleared his throat. "I think we're getting closer," he replied, trying to keep his voice steady.

Charlie nodded, returning her attention to her notes.

He watched in silence as she studied the pages, her brow furrowed in concentration.

Grayson was drawn to Charlie's every move. She was mesmerizing; her piercing brown eyes seemed to stare straight into his soul. He watched as her fingers deftly flipped through the pages of the murder book.

He considered telling her how she made him feel, but he couldn't bring himself to do it. This was not the right time or place. Besides, the cold case had to come first. It was a tough one, and they needed to keep their focus.

As they worked late into the evening, Grayson found himself stealing glances at Charlie whenever he thought she wasn't looking. Never in a million years had he expected to feel anything for her other than maybe friendship.

His eyes shifted upward. *God, are You sure that she's the one for me?*

Grayson caught Charlie's gaze and held it for a moment longer than necessary. He took a deep breath and opened his mouth to speak, but before he could say anything, Charlie spoke up.

"I know we've had our differences in the past, but I want you to know that I respect you as a colleague and as a person," she said, her voice soft and sincere. "I think we make a great team, and I hope that we can continue to work together in the future."

Grayson felt his heart sink. He had finally decided to confess his feelings, only to be met with a professional acknowledgment. He forced a smile and nodded, pretending that he was okay with it.

But deep down, Grayson knew that he wanted more than just a working relationship with Charlie. He wanted her to see him as a man, not just her partner.

TWELVE

"Mrs. Armstrong, what can I do for you?" Charlie asked. She was surprised to find that their unexpected visitor was none other than Joel's wife, Brittany. Grayson appeared just as astonished. Neither of them had thought to hear from her. She didn't seem interested in wanting Joel to talk to them when they visited him at the stadium.

"I thought we should talk," Brittany responded. "Without my husband."

"Sure," Charlie said, then gestured for Grayson to join them in the interview room.

"Did something happen since we last saw you?" Studying her, Charlie was checking for any sign that she was being physically abused. "Did he lay a hand on you?"

Brittany seemed shocked by her question. "No, nothing like that. My husband has never laid a hand on me. And if he did, there won't be any need for the police, except to arrest me for murder."

"Okay," Charlie murmured. "Please…have a seat."

When they were all sitting down at the oblong table, Brittany said, "Joel and I had a long talk after your visit. He told me everything about Melanie. And about her roommate *Kathy Dixon*."

"What about Kathy?" Grayson inquired.

"Joel didn't just have a casual relationship with Melanie. He loved her and had planned on proposing marriage, but she left town without a word to him. When Joel found out where she was, he reached out, but Melanie didn't respond. He told me that's when he realized it was over between them. However, he was later contacted by Kathy. She emailed him, telling him that Melanie was seeing someone. One email turned into another… They met and soon became lovers. Joel said that he was heartbroken and she was basically throwing herself at him. He finally gave in. Initially, he did it to get back at Melanie."

Charlie glanced over at Grayson. This was the first time they were hearing about Kathy and Joel. It dawned on her that this was what Kathy had been hiding. Her relationship with Melanie's ex-boyfriend. This was probably why the two women weren't getting along. She asked, "Did Melanie ever find out?"

"Joel said that she did and was livid," Brittany responded. "She sent him an email. Melanie told him that she intended to confront Kathy about it. She felt it was disrespectful coming from the two of them."

Grayson asked, "Do you think Kathy could have had anything to do with Melanie's death?"

"I honestly don't know anything about the woman. Only what Joel's told me," Brittany replied, "but with everything he said—I wouldn't put it past her. According to my husband, Kathy became obsessive over him. She told him, now that Melanie knew, they could come out into the public with their relationship. But he didn't want to be with her like that. He wasn't over Melanie, so he began ghosting her. He even told Kathy that he'd get a restraining order if she didn't leave him alone."

She pulled a folder out of her designer tote. "Joel kept copies of text and email messages exchanged between them. He said he couldn't trust Kathy so he wanted to protect himself." Brittany handed the folder to Charlie.

"Why are you giving us this information?"

"Joel is innocent. This should help prove it."

"How long have you and Joel been together?" Charlie asked.

"Eleven years together and six of those years as husband and wife," Brittany responded. "I hope you'll do what you can to keep Joel's name out of your investigation. His relationship with Melanie is in the past. We would like for you to leave it there."

"Does Joel know about your visit to see us?"

"My husband and I don't have any secrets," Brittany said.

"We still need to speak with him directly," Grayson stated.

"You're welcome to come to our home for that. Joel is in negotiations for a new contract. He doesn't need accusations of any kind right now."

"Why didn't you want him to give us a DNA sample?" Charlie asked. "Joel didn't have a problem with it."

"I didn't want him to give it to you because I know of cases where DNA has put the wrong person behind bars," Brittany admitted. "I didn't want to take that chance."

After the interview ended and Brittany had left the precinct, Charlie said, "Now, according to Kathy, she'd never met Joel Armstrong. That's clearly a lie—she was sleeping with the man. I'd like to know why Kathy didn't want us to know about her relationship with him."

"It's motive. She wanted Joel, who was probably using her to get to Melanie."

Grayson sat back in his chair, looking deep in thought. The new information Brittany provided had put all their current focus on Kathy. His gut instincts were once again correct.

"I think we should give that note a second look," Charlie stated.

Grayson eyed her. "Do you think Kathy wrote it?"

"Maybe," Charlie responded. "But I know Kathy is right-handed and the author of that note was left-handed." She paused for a moment, then uttered, "Wait a minute…" Charlie went back through the murder book. "Actually…what if Melanie had written the note?" she proposed. "I saw in a medical report that she had surgery on her left hand. I'll investigate when she got that procedure done. It might have been around the time she found out about Kathy and Joel. This would've forced her to use her right hand to write the note."

"Which would throw off her handwriting."

"She leaves the note for her roommate…then there's a confrontation and Kathy murders Melanie." Charlie looked at him. "I want to also talk to Joel about his relationship with Kathy. But I'd like to do it alone. *Just me and him.*"

"You're thinking he'll be more candid if it's just you?"

Charlie nodded. "I do. I'm a woman and I think he'd feel less threatened by me, especially if I'm alone."

Grayson spent the next few hours combing through the information Brittany had given them. Joel and Kathy were involved for a couple of months, it seemed. There was also evidence of jealousy on Kathy's part, including several angry texts to Joel after he ghosted her. Grayson also went through Kathy's social media profiles.

After searching way back, he found a couple of photos from her college days, along with photos of her wearing a Charlotte Bears jersey. The number on it belonged to Joel.

"Kathy claimed not to know the guy but she was wearing his jersey," Grayson stated.

"I wonder if she wore it around Melanie."

"I'm sure she did—it probably gave her some sort of secret thrill," he responded.

Charlie agreed. "I can't wait to get her back here to confront her with everything we've learned so far, but first I want to hear Joel's side."

"You talk to Joel and I'll go see Kathy," Grayson suggested.

"I think she likes you," Charlie teased. "Don't forget that she's a married woman."

"Let's hope that she remembers this," he responded with a chuckle. "I didn't miss the way she kept looking at me when she was here at the precinct."

"I didn't either. I saw the flirty smiles she kept giving you. On second thought, maybe I should go along with you," she offered.

"I can handle Mrs. Kathy Ross."

"Seriously, call me if you need protection."

Grayson burst into laughter.

As he drove to Kathy's house, Grayson's mind raced with questions. Could she really be capable of murder? Was there any evidence linking her to the crime?

When Grayson arrived at Kathy's house, he found her sitting on the porch with a glass of lemonade and a book.

She smiled at him when he joined her. "I had a feeling I'd be seeing you again. Where's Detective Tesarkee?"

"She's taking care of something."

Kathy's smile grew wider. "It's nice to see you again."

"I hope you still feel this way at the end of our conversation."

"If you'd like, we can talk in the house. My mother just took my daughter to the park and my husband is at the office."

"I'm fine right out here on the porch," Grayson stated.

"This shouldn't take long. I just need some clarity on a few things."

"I've told you everything." Kathy paused a moment before asking, "Are you sure that's the only reason you came all the way over here to see me? *Alone.*"

"Positive," Grayson responded. He wasn't falling for her charms or the seductive tone in her voice.

Kathy's smile grew even wider as Grayson sat down in the empty chair beside her.

"Ask me whatever you want."

"Why didn't you ever mention that you and Joel Armstrong were lovers?"

Kathy's smile faltered slightly at Grayson's question. She sat up straight in the chair. She clearly hadn't expected him to bring up Joel so soon.

"Obviously, it's not something I like to talk about," she replied before taking a sip of her lemonade. "Joel and I were a huge mistake. One I wanted to forget. I thought he was falling in love with me, but it turned out he was only using me."

Grayson nodded, studying her face for a moment. "I can understand why it might be difficult to talk about, but I think it's important that you're completely honest with us. It's the only way we'll be able to solve Melanie's murder."

Kathy took a deep breath and looked up at Grayson. "The truth is, I don't think Joel loved anyone but himself. When I first met him, I thought he was passionate and caring, but then I discovered that he also had a dark side. But he has a way of really drawing you in..."

"What are you not telling me?" he asked. "Kathy, I came here to formally arrest you." He'd said it mostly to try to scare her into revealing everything she'd been keeping from them.

It worked because her eyes widened in shock, and tears

streamed down her face. "No, please," she uttered. "I didn't mean for any of this to happen."

"For what to happen?"

"The night Melanie died… I left the door unlocked for Joel. He wanted to see Melanie. He said he needed to talk to her one last time. He wanted to get her out of his system. He said for *us*."

"And you believed him?" Grayson asked.

"I loved him. I thought he'd finally come to his senses and that we'd be together."

His voice was low and serious as he stood up. "Kathy Dixon-Ross, you have the right to remain silent. Anything you say can and will be used against you in a court of law. You have the right to an attorney. If you cannot afford an attorney, one will be provided for you."

"You're kidding, right?"

He heard the panic in her voice, but wouldn't allow it to sway him from doing his job. "I'm afraid not."

More tears sprang into her eyes. "You're arresting me? I didn't do anything! I'm innocent."

"That's to be determined," Grayson said.

This was the break in the case that they had been waiting for, but it also meant that Kathy may have played a role in Melanie's death. He couldn't help but feel a sense of disappointment in knowing he had been right about her.

He called Charlie on the way to let her know that he had Kathy in custody.

She met them at the interrogation room shortly after they had arrived at the precinct.

When they sat down to talk, Kathy said, "I need you to understand that Joel was a part of my past that I wanted to stay buried. It took me a long time to get over him. I thought it was all over until he called me that day. He lied to me."

"When did Melanie find out that you were seeing him behind her back?" Grayson asked.

"I'm not sure," Kathy said. "I came home one day and found a note taped to my bedroom door. It said 'I'm not stupid.'"

"Was it the one we found near her body?" Charlie asked.

"They said the same thing, but there were two different notes. The one Melanie wrote to me—I tore it up that same day. I don't know who wrote the one that was in her room. She and I got into a huge argument over my relationship with Joel. He broke things off and ghosted me after that."

"How did she find out about you and Joel?" Grayson inquired.

"She saw a text from him. I'd left my phone on the kitchen counter. While I was in the shower, she went through my messages. Melanie said she knew I was seeing someone—she thought I was involved with a married man so she decided to be nosey. I'd never seen her so angry." Kathy looked up at Charlie. "It was obvious that she wasn't over Joel. And he claimed to still love her."

"How did that make you feel?" Charlie asked.

Kathy swiped at a tendril of hair that had fallen loose. "How do you think? I was in love with the man. I thought *we* were meant to be together."

"And that's why you left the door unlocked," Charlie uttered.

"Joel said we could be together but first, he had to get Melanie out of his system. He said he needed closure. He could only get that by talking to her."

Grayson gave Kathy a hard stare. "It never crossed your mind that he was the one who killed her?"

"Of course it did," she responded. "It's why I ended things with Joel. I was scared I'd end up the same way."

"So, you're saying that he meant what he'd said about being with you?" Charlie asked.

"I don't think he did, but it didn't matter. I wanted him out of my life at that point."

Charlie played with her pen. "See… I'm not sure I believe you."

Kathy shifted in her seat, her eyes flickering to the two-way mirror. "Joel and I had a connection that I've never felt with anyone else. I knew all about his temper, but I was never afraid of him until the day I found Melanie dead in our apartment."

Grayson leaned forward, his eyes fixed on Kathy. "Tell us about the night Melanie died and don't leave out anything."

Kathy took a deep breath, her hands shaking. "Melanie and I went to the library to study after our classes ended. Things were tense between us, but we lived together and were just trying to get along. She was planning to move out, but I still wanted to fix things between us."

"After betraying her?" Charlie asked. "You just expected her to forgive and forget?"

"I told her the truth. That Joel seduced me. I told her how I'd emailed him just to tell him that I was a fan and I wanted him to sign my jersey. We arranged to meet and he seduced me."

"Try again," Charlie said. "With the truth this time."

Kathy gave her an exasperated look. "I *am* telling the truth."

Grayson flipped open the folder containing the information Brittany had given them. "We have copies of the messages exchanged between you and Joel. They tell a slightly different story."

"Okay, so I went after Joel. He was handsome and rich. There's nothing wrong with that."

"Then why lie about it?" Charlie asked. "You lied to me from the beginning, Kathy. Now, we want the *truth*."

"I asked Melanie to go to the club with me. I was trying to repair our friendship," she stated. "While we were there, I got a text from Joel. That's why I told Melanie that I wasn't feeling well. He wanted to come over so they could talk face-to-face. He didn't want Melanie to know that he was coming."

"What happened next?" Grayson asked.

"Joel asked me to leave the apartment, so I made arrangements to stay with a friend. Then I called him to let him know I really wasn't happy about it. I was afraid that he and Melanie might end up in bed together. He said I had to trust him. He kept insisting that he just wanted to talk to her."

Kathy looked at Charlie. "I looked for Melanie the next day. I wanted to ask how things had gone with Joel. I'd texted him earlier that morning but didn't hear back. When she wasn't on campus, I went home. I opened the door, and the apartment was eerily quiet. I called out to Melanie, but there was no answer, so I decided to check her bedroom. And then I saw her…"

Tears streamed down Kathy's face as she recounted the gruesome details of that day. "She was lying there, on the floor, covered in blood. I was in shock. I didn't know what to do. I called Joel, demanding to know why Melanie was dead. He sounded shocked, then said that he wasn't the one who killed her. He told me that they talked and then he left. Joel made me swear that I'd never tell the police anything about his visit. He told me to take it to the grave. The truth is that I didn't believe him."

Charlie placed a piece of paper in front of Kathy. "Now you can put it all on paper."

"I think I need to speak to an attorney."

Grayson and Charlie left the interrogation room.

"It's time to bring Joel in," he said.

She agreed. "But I'd still like to do this one alone."

Joel's mansion was an impressive example of modern design. Charlie entered the foyer; the floors were made of a dark marble. He led her into a great room filled with musical instruments on display, spanning from floor to ceiling: an instrument from each country he visited. They had passed a room filled with trophies, plaques and pictures of himself in action over the years.

"What do you want from me, Detective?" he spat. "I gave Brittany all the information about Kathy that I had."

"There are some untruths in your story," Charlie growled.

"I have no idea what you're referring to!"

"You made contact with Kathy the night Melanie died."

He looked like a ton of bricks had just been dropped on him, and his breath seemed to get caught up in his chest.

Charlie sensed a sudden change in Joel's demeanor. His face turned pale, and beads of sweat started forming on his forehead. She knew she had struck a nerve, and she had to keep pushing.

"Kathy left the door unlocked to let you inside the apartment. You were the last person to see Melanie alive."

"That's not true."

"Yes, it is," she countered. "When Kathy returned the next day, your ex-girlfriend was dead. Why did you kill her? Was it because she didn't want to take you back?"

"You don't know what you're talking about, lady."

Charlie stared at Joel with a fierce intensity, refusing to back down. She knew she was onto something. It was in his eyes, the way they flicked back and forth, searching for a way out. But there was no escape, not anymore. Charlie had cornered him.

"Melanie once filed an abuse charge against you, didn't she?" Charlie was bluffing once again, trying to see if her gut instinct was correct. The more she thought about it, the more she believed that Joel had either hit Melanie or come pretty close to it.

He glared at her.

"But somehow you got her to drop the charges. Melanie did what you wanted but then she left town."

"You don't know what you're talking about," Joel repeated.

"Oh, I know exactly what I'm talking about," Charlie said, taking a step closer to him. "And I'm not going to stop until you're held accountable for your actions."

Joel smirked, a dangerous glint in his eyes. "And what are you going to do about it?" he sneered, rising to his feet.

Charlie pulled out her weapon, stopping him in his tracks.

Joel's face twisted into a snarl. "You think you scare me?" he spat. "I'm not afraid of a woman with a gun."

Charlie's grip on the gun tightened; she quickly switched the safety off, her finger hovering over the trigger. "Try me," she said.

Joel's face hardened with anger as he stared at her, the air around them thickening with tension. His chuckle sent a chill down Charlie's spine and she quickly steeled herself against him. "You won't get away with this," he said, advancing closer.

Charlie could feel her heart pounding in her chest as she leveled the gun toward Joel. "I said stay back!" she yelled, her voice shaking only slightly despite the fear racing through her body.

But Joel kept coming, his hands grasping for the gun.

Without hesitation, Charlie fired off a warning shot next to him and screamed, "Try that again and I won't miss!"

Joel stumbled back, shock and disbelief painted across his face. "This is harassment," he spat out incredulously.

"No," Charlie answered firmly, keeping the gun trained on him while also reaching for her handcuffs with her other hand. "This is where I arrest you and take you down to the precinct. Keep your hands up where I can see them."

But Joel shook his head. "Look, I wasn't gonna hurt you… You don't have to do this."

Charlie cocked her head to one side but kept the gun aimed at him. "Actually, I do. Joel Armstrong, you have the right to remain silent," Charlie stated. "Anything you say can and will be used against you in a court of law. You have the right to an attorney. If you cannot afford an attorney, one will be provided for you."

"I can't believe this," he uttered along with a string of profanity. "Kat and that big mouth of hers…she knows that I didn't kill Melanie."

THIRTEEN

Grayson burst through the door of the interrogation room, his eyes aflame. He stepped in with determination, pointing a threatening finger at Joel.

"I heard you tried to attack Detective Tesarkee," he growled out between gritted teeth. "Now, I suggest you answer her questions."

"You don't have to keep these on me," Joel stated, nodding toward the handcuffs around his wrists.

"Oh, I don't know..." Grayson responded. "I like the metal bracelets on you."

Joel bristled at his words but remained silent.

He sat down beside Charlie.

"Are you willing to discuss what happened that night?" she asked.

"Doesn't look like I have any choice," Joel huffed. "I might as well get this over with, so yeah... I don't have a problem talking to y'all. You're wrong though. I didn't hurt the one woman I loved more than my own life."

"You're referring to Melanie and not your wife, right?" Grayson interjected.

Joel sent a sharp glare in his direction.

"Tell us in your words what happened then," Charlie said.

"Yeah, I reached out to Kat because I wanted to get into

the apartment so that I could speak to Melanie. I didn't tell her to leave the door unlocked or anything like that, that was all her idea. I just wanted her to let me in."

"How did Melanie respond?" Charlie questioned. "Was she excited or annoyed?"

"She was surprised to see me, but she wasn't angry. We had a good conversation. I apologized for everything that happened between us. I told her how things went down with Kat and how I had no feelings for the woman." Joel paused a moment, then said, "I told Melanie that I still loved her and would do anything to get her back."

"And how did she respond to that?" Grayson asked.

"Melanie said that she still loved me too, but she'd read in the tabloids that I was dating someone. I told her that I'd end it with Brittany. We kissed and I thought we were going to make love, but then Melanie changed her mind. She said she didn't want to make a mistake by rushing. She wanted to take her time."

Grayson eyed Joel. "And did you just let it go at that?"

"Yeah," he answered. "I wanted to spend the rest of my life with Melanie. I'd messed up with her twice and so I was willing to do this however she wanted."

"Joel, what did you expect to happen after that night?" Charlie inquired.

He let out a deep sigh. "Well, I was going to end things with Brittany. It wouldn't have been easy—she was gonna be furious, but I knew that Melanie was the one for me. We were going to start seeing each other again. Things were gonna be different. She was hesitant to take things further, and I wasn't gonna push her."

Grayson nodded in understanding. "I get it. You didn't want to make the same mistake twice and lose her again."

"Exactly," Joel said with a grimace. "But it was hard. I wanted to keep going."

Charlie smirked. "So why didn't you?"

Joel's cheeks turned red. "I didn't want to make her uncomfortable. I didn't want to come across as desperate. I figured I'd give her space and wait for her to come around. I just knew all the way to my soul that we were going to work out this time, but then someone took her away from me."

"When did you find out Melanie was dead?" Grayson asked.

"Kat called me the following day. She accused me of killing Melanie," Joel said. "We argued because I figured she might have come home and they had a fight or something."

"Over you," Charlie uttered.

"Look, I wasn't happy about it," he responded. "I was angry with Kat. I warned her that if she'd done anything to Melanie..." His voice trailed off.

"You threatened her," Grayson said.

"I just made it clear that I'd see Kat punished if she was the one who killed Melanie. When I said it, I was talking about the police. I would've gone to the cops and told them everything."

"I don't believe that at all," Charlie stated. "You made threats to make sure that Kathy kept your name out of the investigation, Joel. That's the truth."

"I would've found a way to make sure Kat was punished for her crime."

She met his gaze. "It was you who sent that email. You said you knew who had murdered Melanie. Why did you change your mind about Kathy?"

"I just realized that she wasn't capable of doing something so heinous," Joel responded. "I didn't think she had the stomach for it. Kat couldn't stand the sight of blood. I remember how she almost passed out one time when I had a nosebleed. It grossed her out something terrible."

"Did you break things off with Brittany?" Grayson asked.

"Yeah. The next day."

"How did she take it?"

"She was hurt and angry, of course," Joel responded. "But after Melanie died…we decided to try again. You know, I'm tired of talking to y'all. It's time I tell you that I want my attorney."

"We have both of them in custody," Charlie stated. "And at least we now know the identity of our unknown witness/suspect."

Grayson agreed. "I'm really leaning toward Joel for this. I don't believe Melanie was as forgiving as he'd like us to think. She had strong feelings about domestic violence."

She sat down behind her desk. "You think that Melanie refused him that night and he got upset, which escalated. When Joel realized what he'd done—he left the apartment."

"That's my theory."

Charlie reached for a file on her desk and flipped it open. "We've got a strong case against him, but we need to make sure we have all our ducks in a row before we present it to the district attorney. Mainly because we don't have any witnesses to put him at the apartment. No one saw anything that night. Kathy didn't see him there. We can make it stronger if we find someone who could maybe place Joel at the scene."

Taking a seat in a visitor chair which faced her desk, Grayson contemplated for a moment. "What about Melanie's neighbor? We can interview her again."

Charlie nodded. "Let's revisit Tabitha and continue trying to contact the other neighbors. Maybe they remember something now that they didn't before." She felt a huge surge of confidence that their investigation was coming together and getting closer to an answer.

"I really feel good about the direction this investigation is taking," she said.

"For the most part, so do I," Grayson responded. "But there's a part of me that feels like we're still missing something important."

The phone on Charlie's desk rang.

"That was a police detective in Florida. There's no point in looking for Tobias Jacobs anymore," she said, after hanging up. "He died two years ago but his body wasn't identified until late last year. He was a John Doe."

"Was he murdered?" Grayson asked.

"No, he was homeless and was found dead in a tent. He had a heart attack and apparently had been dead for several days before anyone even took notice."

"That's too bad," he responded.

Charlie took a moment to remember the young man. She felt bad that he'd died alone like that—no one had even known his name. He was simply a John Doe.

"Back to the Joel and his wife. Where was Brittany that night?"

Grayson's question drew her out of her thoughts. She looked at him. "What are you thinking?"

"This is just a theory, but what if Brittany followed Joel that night? Maybe she decided to confront Melanie after he left. Maybe it was Brittany who was heartbroken and filled with a jealous rage."

"Enough for her to stab someone to death," Charlie said. "It's definitely possible. We need to see if she has an alibi."

"Want to take a ride?" he asked. "I want to do this face-to-face."

* * *

This investigation was pulling them closer together professionally and personally. Grayson was careful to avoid letting his growing attraction interfere with their common goal to find the person responsible for Melanie's death.

As soon as they stepped outside the precinct, Charlie stood face-to-face with the man Grayson had seen her speaking with outside the deli. Her father.

"Sam, what are you doing here?" she asked, her voice full of both surprise and dread.

"I'm not here for you," he responded. "I came down to help a friend of mine. He was picked up last night for drunk and disorderly conduct."

"Oh."

"I am glad to see you though."

"I have to run out, but I'm glad you're there for your friend. It's really interesting, since you weren't there for your own daughter when she needed you the most."

"Charlotte…"

"Bye, Sam."

They walked to the car in silence.

"Well, that was my father," Charlie said after climbing inside. "I hadn't seen him for years until a couple weeks ago and then today. He's an alcoholic…well, he said that he's been clean for almost two years. I have no idea if he's telling the truth."

"Where's your mom?"

"She died a while back. She drank as much as he did if not more. When she died…that's when he did a total disappearing act. I was in foster care, so it was easy for him to just forget about me." She glanced over at Grayson. "I didn't grow up like the Brady Bunch or the Cosbys. I basically had to raise myself until CPS took me out of the home."

"I wasn't in the system," he responded. "But like me… you're a survivor. You're determined not to let your past define your future."

"It's funny how I always imagined you born with a silver spoon in your mouth," Charlie said. "You were always talking about your travels, the best hotels, food…designer this and that. Your close-knit family."

"I did do those things with family, but with a family from church who embraced me. That was the life I'd created for myself," Grayson replied as he pulled into the circular driveway and parked.

Before they could get out of the car all the way, Brittany rushed outside. "Why are you here? I gave you everything."

"I have a question for you," Charlie said. "Where were you the night Melanie was murdered?"

Brittany glared at her. "I was at my house. Joel was there with me."

Charlie shook her head no. "That's not what we were told by your husband."

Brittany's gaze went from Charlie to Grayson. "Where is Joel? I've been calling him and it's going straight to voice mail."

"He's at the precinct. He's been arrested," Charlie answered.

"For what?"

"Melanie's murder. He and Kathy both were arrested."

Looking confused, Brittany frowned. "I don't understand. What happened?"

"Your husband wanted to see Melanie, so Kathy left the door unlocked so that he could get into the apartment."

Her eyes rose in surprise. "That can't be right."

"They both gave a statement saying as much," Charlie said.

"Joel was here when I went to sleep that night. And now

you believe he killed her? You wouldn't be here at my house if you didn't."

"We're just verifying everything we've been told," Grayson said.

"Did Joel request an attorney?"

"Yeah, but only after he made his statement," Charlie responded.

"Joel told you that he saw Melanie the night she was murdered?" Brittany asked.

"Yes," Charlie replied.

Brittany shook her head in disbelief. "I need to see him… talk to him. I'm his attorney. He never should've spoken to you without me."

"She's angry," Charlie commented when they walked out to the car. "I don't know if she's mad with her husband or us."

"Probably both," Grayson responded. "Going back to what we talked about earlier… I won't tell anyone at the precinct about your dad. It stays between us. Your secret is safe with me."

Charlie smiled. "Thank you." After a moment, she said, "I feel like I've never known you at all until now. You're not anything like I thought."

"I used to be," Grayson said with a chuckle. "I was a narcissist. I believed my own press, but God had His way of getting my attention. He could've let me die the night of the accident. The doctors told me that I almost did die a couple of times, but He allowed me to live. That was one of the most terrifying moments of my life, Charlie. And I don't scare easily."

She glimpsed his eyes filling with water and reached over to take his hand. "God was there when you needed Him the most," Charlie said. "I don't think He sees me at all."

His heart was saddened by her words. Grayson swiped at his eyes, then responded, "He sees you and He loves you."

"He didn't hear my prayers so I stopped praying."

"I'm sure He speaks to you all the time—you just don't recognize His voice."

His cell phone rang.

"I need to take this." He turned away from Charlie and reached for his phone.

"That was Valerie Nobles," Grayson announced when he hung up the phone a few minutes later. "The neighbor who lived across the hall from Kathy and Melanie. She's coming to Charlotte…flying in tonight. She's coming to the precinct tomorrow morning."

Charlie smiled. "That's great. I hope she'll be able to tell us something to help the case further."

Then Grayson abruptly changed the topic by saying, "Come to church with me on Sunday."

She glanced away for a moment, as if unsure of how to respond. The silence stretched between them before she spoke. "Thank you for the invitation, but I'd rather not."

Though disappointment briefly coursed through him, he didn't press her. He simply nodded and silently prayed that one day she would accept his invite.

FOURTEEN

Jen surprised Charlie with a meal from a small family-owned eatery located a couple blocks from where she lived.

"Thank you for dinner," she said. "I'm going to be here late." She opened the take-out container and began eagerly scooping up forkfuls of chicken fricassee.

"I heard you and Grayson may have found the person who killed Melanie Goins," Jen stated. "Congratulations."

"I feel really good about the arrests. I just wish I could place the weapon in Joel Armstrong's hand. We requested a search warrant."

"Do you really think you'll find it in his house?"

Charlie wiped her mouth with a paper napkin. "No, but there's a chance."

"True."

"So, you and Grayson seem to be working well together," Jen said after a pause.

"I already know where this is going," she said. "Jen… stop trying to find me a man. You know I have trust issues."

"Stop trying to use that as an excuse. Just take a chance. God didn't create us to be alone. Besides, Grayson is a really nice guy."

"But that doesn't mean we're supposed to be together."

"I've known you both for a very long time," Jen stated.

"You're attracted to him and he's attracted to you as well. I can see it all over both your faces."

Charlie concentrated on her food. She wanted to put an end to this discussion. She wanted to continue ignoring whatever she felt for Grayson. It wasn't a wise decision to tamper with their already fragile working relationship by mixing in other emotions. Best to keep it platonic. However, the more time she spent with Grayson, the more challenging it became to keep her feelings at bay.

"How do you feel about the detective II exam?" she asked to shift the direction of their conversation.

"I think I'm ready," Jen answered. "I took those college classes Kyle suggested. He's been great about helping me reach my goals. Out of all of my supervisors—he's the best I've had."

"Phillipa's good about stuff like that, too. She wants to see us go as far as we can within the department. I appreciate her giving me this second chance to close Melanie's case. I really don't want to let her down, especially since Commander Peters didn't think it was a good idea. She really had my back on this. I can't fail."

Jen smiled at her. "You won't. You have two suspects in custody. You know more about the case than you did eleven years ago. You've got this."

Charlie sliced into her chicken. "You're right. I have my person. I just have to make sure my case is airtight."

Although she tried to project confidence, deep down she was plagued with doubt. The inner voice kept warning her that this situation was more complicated than it seemed on the surface.

Valerie Nobles-Hardwick was escorted to the interview room shortly after nine o'clock.

"Thanks so much for coming," Charlie said, admiring the expensive pantsuit on the woman's full-figured frame.

"I came to town for business," Valerie stated. She sat down and placed her designer bag in the empty chair beside her. "I wasn't aware that Melanie's case had been reopened until I checked my messages and there was one from a Detective Leigh."

"We've been trying to reach you for a couple weeks."

"I was out of the country. On my *honeymoon*. I didn't want to be disturbed."

Charlie nodded. "He'll be joining us shortly." Grayson was talking with Kathy's husband, explaining why his wife had been arrested.

"I'd like to go over the events of the night Melanie died."

"I figured as much," Valerie responded as she played with the huge diamond on her ring finger.

Charlie glanced down at the notes Grayson had given her. Valerie was a sports agent. She represented athletes.

"Can we get started? I have a meeting with a client in two hours."

"Sure."

The door opened and Grayson entered.

"We were just about to begin," Charlie said.

He introduced himself to Valerie before taking his seat.

"Like I told you that night, I saw Melanie and Kathy from time to time—I was in grad school and working. I wouldn't say we were friends, but we would talk."

"So, you never socialized with them?" Grayson asked.

"No, I didn't."

"What can you tell me about their relationship?"

"Not a whole lot," Valerie answered, looking straight at him. She seemed to have dismissed Charlie's presence. "I would say that they had some problems, but they weren't the only ones. It can be hit-or-miss with roommates."

"You had a roommate, I recall," Charlie stated. "But he wasn't in town the night Melanie died."

"He'd moved out the week before she was killed," Valerie responded. "Even before he moved, Lucas was hardly home. He worked as a flight attendant. I considered him the perfect roommate."

"Lucas Shelby," Charlie said. "I didn't get a chance to speak with him back then. Do you know where he's currently living?"

"I don't. He moved away to be with some woman. After that fizzled out, I didn't hear anything else. He wouldn't have been any help anyway. He hardly ever really saw them because of his schedule. When he was at home, he kept to himself mostly."

"Did you hear anything that night?" Grayson asked. "Your apartment was right across from theirs."

"I heard two people arguing. I just assumed it was Kathy and Melanie. I'd heard them before," Valerie said.

"Could you make out any of the words during the argument?" Charlie asked.

"Now that you mention it, I think one of them said something about a man…or *my man*… At least that's what it sounded like."

"Anything else?" she prompted.

"*You'll never have him*... I don't know for sure," Valerie said. "For all I know, it might have been the television. It was turned up pretty loud."

"Did you hear any screams?" Grayson asked.

"I put in my earphones. I was trying to study for an exam. I did that whenever there were parties or people being loud." Valerie paused a moment, then said, "I looked out the window about twenty, thirty minutes later and I saw a woman rushing to her car. I noticed her because I really liked her car—it was a brand-new convertible Mercedes-Benz. It was a gorgeous black color. I remember it because it was my dream car."

"Did you recognize this woman?"

Valerie shook her head no. "There wasn't anything special about her, but I knew she didn't live in the complex and I don't know who she was visiting."

Charlie swallowed her frustration. Instead of the case getting easier, it seemed to become more convoluted.

"I do remember her blond hair peeking from the hat she was wearing."

"Did you say blond hair?" Grayson asked.

"Yes, does it mean something?" Valerie questioned.

"It might," he said.

They finished up their conversation with Valerie.

When she was gone, Charlie said, "I'm checking to see if Brittany or Joel drove a convertible Mercedes back then."

Minutes later, she and Grayson had their answer.

"She lied about being home asleep," Charlie stated. "She knew Joel had left the house because she followed him to the apartment."

"Do you think she was the one who killed Melanie?" Grayson asked.

"If Brittany heard Joel confessing his love to her—it might have sent her into a jealous rage."

Grayson nodded in agreement, his mind already racing with possible motives and scenarios. "We need to bring her in for questioning," he said, his voice low and serious. "She told us she was home that night—now we know she was at the apartment complex."

Charlie had a feeling that this wasn't going to be as easy

as simply bringing Brittany in and getting a confession out of her.

As they made their way to the Armstrong estate, Charlie was sure they had finally caught their killer.

When they arrived at the house, Brittany seemed surprised to see them. "Is everything okay?" she asked, looking nervous.

"We just have a few more questions for you," Grayson said, his tone calm and collected.

They sat down in Brittany's living room, and Charlie watched as Grayson took the lead in questioning her.

"I don't know what else I can tell you about that night. Joel didn't kill Melanie. She was alive when he left her apartment."

"How do you know that?" he asked.

Brittany shifted her position in the chair she was sitting in. "He told me and I believe him."

"You knew he left the house that night. You knew because you followed him."

"I don't know what you're talking about."

"Brittany, you were seen leaving the building. A witness identified the car you were driving back then," Grayson stated. "The convertible Mercedes-Benz Cabriolet E350 that Joel bought you for your birthday."

"This conversation has come to an end," she responded. "I want my lawyer."

"That's a very wise decision because I have a warrant for your arrest," he said before reciting her Miranda rights.

Charlie opened the door to allow the officers waiting outside to enter. "They're here to search your house."

"You won't find anything here," Brittany stated. "Search away…"

Charlie led her out of the house in handcuffs.

"The media is going to have a field day with this," Brittany uttered. "Joel and I will be suing the police department…you can count on it. We didn't do this. We didn't murder anyone."

"Then you should've told us the truth the first time," Charlie stated. "People lie when they have something to hide."

"You've just messed with the wrong people. I'm going after your badges for this."

"Watch your head," Charlie said as she ushered her into the backseat of the car.

She got into the front passenger seat while Grayson was in the driver's seat.

The car ride was silent; the only sound was Brittany's heavy breathing.

Charlie was sure the woman's mind was racing, thinking about how her life had turned upside down in a matter of minutes.

"My reputation will be destroyed by this," Brittany said, "My father warned me that I couldn't trust Joel, but I wouldn't listen. Now I'm paying the price for my mistake. I'm in this mess because of *him*. All I've done is protect him—protect his reputation. No more…"

The car pulled up to the police station, and Charlie got out to open the door for Brittany.

"The media's already out here."

"Most likely it's because of Joel's arrest."

"I'm not stupid," Brittany snapped.

Charlie paused to look at her before helping her out of the car. They were immediately met with a barrage of flashing cameras. Brittany tried to shield her eyes as she walked toward the building.

"I'm going to see that you both pay for this."

Charlie turned Brittany over to another police officer. "Take Mrs. Armstrong to Booking."

* * *

"She's lawyered up," Grayson said. "Maybe it's because she's guilty."

"I wish we could find the murder weapon," Charlie stated. "We need that knife."

"She wouldn't have kept it. Brittany would've gotten rid of it that night."

"Things must have gotten really ugly between the two of them." Charlie shook her head sadly. "She killed Melanie because Joel loved her. He was going to leave Brittany. When Valerie said that she heard arguing—it was Brittany and Melanie that she heard. I don't think it was Kathy."

"She lied to you from the beginning," Grayson said. "She left the door unlocked so that Joel could walk right inside."

"Kathy had no idea that Melanie would end up dead. I don't even think Joel is the guilty party here. It's Brittany."

He agreed. "I don't think we're going to find the knife though. Not in that house. Remember what she said—Brittany told us that we wouldn't find anything."

"Grayson, she could be bluffing."

"I don't think so," he responded. "She sounded almost arrogant about it."

Charlie shrugged. "I believe we can make the charges stick without the knife. She sat in the backseat spouting how she was going to make us pay—she's the one who is going to pay for Melanie's death."

FIFTEEN

Charlie sat down at her desk and began on the paperwork that had to be sent over to the district attorney's office. She and Grayson were both thrilled with the investigation, but there was some unease on her part.

Kathy had been released, but Joel and his wife were still in custody.

She kept thinking about the voice in her head telling her that there was more to this case.

How much more?

Charlie got up and walked away from her desk.

She needed to take a break.

When she returned ten minutes later, she found a message waiting for her. There was a hit on Lucas Shelby.

Charlie signaled for Grayson to come over.

"What's up?" he asked.

"We got a hit on Lucas Shelby. His DNA was obtained during a DUI traffic stop in Raleigh. It matches the DNA taken from the wine bottle. Valerie gave me the impression that he'd left North Carolina."

"It's possible she didn't know where he was," Grayson responded.

"As far as I'm concerned…everybody connected to Melanie is a suspect."

"Are we heading to Raleigh?" he asked.

"Yes," Charlie said.

When they were inside the car, Grayson said, "According to Valerie's statement, Lucas didn't really know Melanie. Yet, there's an expensive bottle of wine with his DNA on it."

"They must have had a conversation or two," Charlie said. "Or maybe he wanted to get to know Melanie and that's why he gave her a bottle of wine."

"Maybe it's just that. He gave her the wine. She was drinking it on the night she died. Melanie was interrupted by Joel and then by his wife," Grayson stated. "There are two scenarios here… Joel killed Melanie. Brittany found her dead and to keep Joel from leaving her—she protects his secret."

"But maybe it was Brittany who killed Melanie when Melanie confronted her about Joel," Charlie suggested. "Valerie told us that she heard what sounded like *you'll never have him*. That means it couldn't have been Joel—it had to be his wife."

"I'm not totally convinced yet," he said. "It's still possible Brittany got there first. She might have found out that Joel wanted to be with Melanie and the two women argued…then Brittany left right before Joel arrived."

"You really think Joel murdered Melanie."

Grayson sighed. "I'm considering all possibilities, Charlie. Between Kathy, Brittany and Joel…he seems the most logical."

"That's why I'm not so sure he did it," she responded. "For all we know, Spring could be a suspect. She low-key pointed fingers at Kathy."

"She didn't like the woman," he said.

"But that doesn't mean she's not capable of murder," Charlie said, tapping her finger against her chin.

Grayson raised an eyebrow. "Are you really considering that Spring killed Melanie?"

"You can't deny that it's a possibility," Charlie replied, shrugging her shoulders. "I mean, think about it. Spring might have been jealous of Melanie's relationship with Kathy. Maybe she thought she was being replaced in the friend department. It's not that far-fetched."

He couldn't help but agree.

"You know...what if it was Lucas?" Grayson asked. "What if he was hiding somewhere waiting for the chance to be with Melanie. He could've heard everything that was said that night. He might have noticed that Kathy left the door unlocked. Maybe he slipped inside without Melanie knowing. Then before he could do anything—Joel shows up. He overhears their conversation. Doesn't like what he hears.

"After Joel leaves, Brittany shows up...she and Melanie argue over Joel. By this time Lucas is enraged. Once Brittany leaves, he attacks Melanie after she rebuffs him. Valerie was absorbed in her studies—it's possible that she didn't know he was in the building at the time."

Charlie considered his theory. "It's plausible." Shaking her head, she said, "This case isn't getting any easier to solve. While you were talking, I kept thinking back to our conversation with Valerie. If you're right, then do you think it's possible that she lied to protect him?"

"It's definitely possible," Grayson responded. "All of these people have been lying to protect someone else—instead of helping us with the answers we need to solve this crime."

"It angers me," Charlie stated. "Melanie deserves better than this from all of them. This is exactly why I don't care to have a lot of friends."

Grayson nodded in agreement. "It's a shame that people

can be so selfish. We're supposed to be a society that looks out for one another, and yet time and time again, we see individuals putting their own interests ahead of others."

Charlie sighed, running her fingers through her hair in frustration. "I just wish we could get someone to talk. Someone who knows something and isn't afraid to come forward with the truth."

Grayson glanced over at Charlie; he could see the exhaustion etched in her face. Charlie had been working tirelessly on the case, and it was starting to take its toll.

"I know it's frustrating," he said, trying to offer some comfort to his partner. "But we'll keep digging. We'll find solid answers soon. We're getting close. I can feel it."

They drove to the address that Lucas had given the police in Raleigh.

He opened the front door, apparently on his way out when they pulled up in front of the house. Grayson parked the vehicle and got out.

"Mr. Shelby, we'd like to talk to you."

"Who are you?" Lucas asked.

"I'm Detective Leigh and this is Detective Tesarkee," Grayson said. "We're investigating the death of Melanie Goins."

"I remember that case. The woman that was killed used to live right across from me."

"That's why we're here," Charlie stated.

"I'm afraid I can't help you," he said, stepping aside to let them enter the house. "I didn't know Melanie or her roommate other than to say hello the few times I saw them. I'd already moved away by the time she was killed."

They sat down in the dining room.

"Lucas, we need you to be honest with us," Grayson said. "You say that you really didn't know Melanie. Can you tell me how your fingerprints ended up on a wine bottle in Melanie's apartment?"

He looked perplexed. "I don't know. I'd never been inside her place."

"Are you saying that you didn't give her the wine?"

Lucas nodded. "That's exactly what I'm saying. I didn't know her like that. Besides, I'm not a wine drinker. Beer was more my style."

"How long have you lived in Raleigh?" Charlie asked.

"I just moved here not even a month ago."

Grayson glanced over at her before inquiring, "Where were you before moving back to North Carolina?"

"I was in Dallas. I switched airlines last month, so I'm based out of RDU now."

"The problem we're having is the fact that your DNA was all over the wine bottle," Grayson stated.

"I don't know what to tell you… I was in Paris the night Melanie died. I remember because Valerie called to tell me about it the next day—I was in shock. I couldn't believe something that horrific happened in the building. She seemed nice enough and didn't have a lot of people over there."

Charlie and Grayson exchanged a glance as Lucas spoke. They had been interviewing him for over thirty minutes but they couldn't find anything that could point to a motive as to why he'd want Melanie dead.

But Charlie sensed that Lucas was hiding something.

"Lucas, I don't believe that you're telling us everything," Charlie said, leaning forward in her seat.

"What do you mean?" Lucas asked, his eyes darting around the room.

"You said you didn't know Melanie all that well. But you seem to know something about her—you thought she was nice enough. I have a feeling that you have had at least one conversation with her," Charlie said. "Were you at the apartment that night?"

Lucas started to fidget in his seat.

"Tell us what happened," Grayson said, his voice stern.

Lucas took a deep breath before he spoke. "Okay, fine. I went to my old apartment to pick up the last of my stuff. I'd left some clothes in the closet. I saw Joel Armstrong coming down the stairs as I was going up. I pretended not to recognize him because he looked upset. I figured he was leaving Melanie's place—I'd heard they dated in college."

"How did you hear that?" Charlie asked.

"I… I'm not sure."

"Did Melanie tell you?"

Lucas eyed Grayson. "No, she didn't. I told you that I didn't know her like that. We weren't friends. We were barely neighbors."

"See…" Charlie murmured. "I think you know much more than you're saying. Do you think that Melanie deserved to die the way she did?"

"No, not at all," he responded.

"Then help us get the person responsible."

Lucas nodded. "When I was leaving, I did see a blond woman get out of a black Mercedes and enter the building. I didn't know who she was until I saw her with Joel in one of the tabloids. I'm not saying that they did anything."

"We understand," Grayson said.

"I don't want to be involved in any of this."

"Then why didn't you contact the police department? You knew we were looking for any information about that night," Charlie said.

"I realized that I could be wrong about my suspicions. I didn't want an innocent person going to prison because of me. I decided it was best if I just stayed out of it."

"Is there anything else?" Grayson asked.

"I heard Valerie and Tabitha talking about Melanie. They said she liked going to wineries and wine tastings. I think one of her uncles was a wine collector or something. But like I said, I don't care for the stuff." He paused a moment, then said, "How did you find me?"

"The DUI stop."

"Oh," Lucas uttered. "That's why I stopped drinking." After a moment, he said, "If that's everything, I'm supposed to meet up with a friend and now I'm running late."

"We'll let you know if we need anything else from you," Charlie stated. "One more question for you—do you have family in Charlotte?"

"Not anymore. I had a brother who lived in Harrisburg, but he died a long time ago. Actually, two weeks before Melanie. Why?"

"Just curious. Thanks for your time."

SIXTEEN

Grayson released a sigh of relief. "I think that's what we need to keep both Joel and his wife in custody. I hope we can get them to turn on one another—that's the only way we'll get to the truth. One of them killed Melanie."

"Lucas said when Joel left, he looked upset," Charlie responded. "This isn't how a man would look if he's getting back with the love of his life. He should have been happy."

He nodded. "Since we're speculating, my theory is that Melanie wasn't at all happy to see Joel. His version of events is another lie."

"But Brittany wouldn't have known that," she suggested. "Maybe she assumed the worst—this could've provoked her to attack Melanie."

"If that's true, then Joel has no idea that his wife murdered the woman he loved."

"He does now," Charlie stated. "As much as I don't care for him—he just might be innocent." She put her hands to her face. "This just isn't making any sense. We're jumping from one person to the next."

"What is your gut telling you?" Grayson asked.

"Joel seems the most likely suspect," she responded. "The person who killed Melanie was filled with rage."

"According to his new attorney, Joel's going to sue the

police department," Grayson said. "He's naming us in the lawsuit."

Charlie shrugged in nonchalance. "That's the least of my worries. We were doing our job."

He felt the same way about the potential litigation. He wasn't going to let the threat of a lawsuit deter him from conducting a thorough investigation.

The drive back to Charlotte took almost three and a half hours due to traffic delays on the freeway.

When they got back to the precinct, they met with Phillipa in her office.

Grayson updated her on their conversation with Lucas.

"There's still the huge question mark on how his prints ended up on a bottle of expensive wine," Phillipa said.

"He's adamant that he didn't give her the wine and that he's never been in her apartment, so I've been thinking about that," Charlie responded. "The hit came from the database. He recently got a DUI."

"Does Lucas have family in the area?" Phillipa questioned.

"I asked. He had a brother in Harrisburg, who died just two weeks before Melanie passed away," she remarked. "My mind is buzzing with questions so I plan to do more research as soon as I return to my desk."

Phillipa nodded in agreement. "Release Brittany Armstrong, but Joel remains in custody for now."

"I'll get back to you with my findings."

Charlie walked out ahead of Grayson. They stood in the hallway talking.

"If Lucas's brother hadn't died before Melanie, I'd be hauling him in here. I never expected this case to be so complicated," she said.

"I still think it's Joel, but we have to cover all of our bases," Grayson stated.

They sat down at her desk.

Minutes later, Charlie pointed to her screen. "Here it is… Leon Shelby. He was reported missing by a friend of his, but his body was found the next day. Cause of death was a knife wound to the heart." She glanced over at Grayson. "His death was never solved. The case is actually here in the CCU. Jen was the detective on record."

Grayson picked up the phone. "Hey, Jen, are you here at the precinct? Come to Charlie's desk when you get a minute."

"I've requested his file," she said when he hung up.

"You don't think…"

"I don't know what to think right now," Charlie said. "Not until we look at everything."

"What's up, my two favorite people?" Jen asked.

"What do you remember about the Leon Shelby murder?" she asked her friend.

"I never found the person responsible. The victim worked as a bartender at an upscale restaurant uptown. Didn't seem to be a troublemaker. He was stabbed with a fixed blade knife…"

Charlie felt a quiver in her belly. "Are you sure?" She couldn't help but wonder if the two cases were somehow related.

Jen nodded.

"Was the weapon ever recovered?" Grayson asked.

"No. CSI suggested that it might have been a custom-designed Ka-Bar knife with serrated edges on the top."

Charlie and Grayson glanced at one another.

"What?" Jen asked. "Is it the same as the knife used in the Goins murder?"

"The one used to kill Melanie didn't have serrated edges," Charlie responded. She still felt they were connected.

After Jen left, Grayson asked, "What are you thinking?"

"I can't tell you how I know—but there's a link between these murders. We just have to fit the pieces together."

"Are you considering two random murders connected by one killer?"

"Naw, I think it goes deeper than that," Charlie said. "Lucas lived across from Melanie and Kathy. I'm sure his brother must have visited him at least once. What if he met Melanie—she was a beautiful woman. Remember she told Spring about some guy she'd met—maybe it was Leon."

"Then Leon was murdered," Grayson said. "That would explain why she suddenly didn't want to talk about him anymore. Why she'd tell Spring that it was over before it really started. She didn't know him long enough to really grieve for him, but she would be upset over his death."

"During the initial investigation, some of her friends, including Spring, said that Melanie seemed bothered by something before she died. Kathy thought it was about her—but maybe it had nothing to do with her at all. It also makes sense why she wouldn't tell Kathy anything about Leon. Especially after Kathy had betrayed her with Joel."

"He was a bartender. He knew she liked wine. Maybe Leon gifted her the bottle of wine…"

"Which could explain the familial DNA," Charlie stated. "Still, there's the DNA found under Melanie's nails. If it comes back with Joel's or Brittany's DNA…we will have our killer."

"We should know something soon. They agreed to give samples." Grayson shifted his position in the chair. "Then there's the connection to the wine bottle…we might have to consider that Joel murdered not just Melanie, but also Leon."

"There weren't any text messages between them on Melanie's phone. We checked the numbers…" She paused. "Wait… there was an IP phone number in the history. It was one of those Google Voice phone numbers. It looked like she used that number for the tutoring she did on the side."

"Sounds like a great place to start," Grayson said, standing to his full height. "I'll work on that."

"I'm going to give Lucas a call."

"Lucas, I have one quick question for you," Charlie said. "Did your brother ever come to visit you while you were living across from Melanie?"

"Yeah, he did. Why?"

"Do you know if they ever met?"

"I would see them talking from time to time, so yeah. Leon was a people person. He never met a stranger." He paused a moment, then asked, "What does this have to do with Melanie's murder?"

"Your brother was murdered a few weeks earlier. He was stabbed to death," Charlie said. "Melanie was also stabbed to death. I believe there's a connection."

Lucas didn't say anything.

"You there?" she prompted.

"Yeah. It's just that we always thought it was some random attack. Leon liked to venture off alone. Go hiking or biking all alone. I didn't even know he was missing. His friend called because they had plans to go to New York that weekend. He said Leon was supposed to be bringing this woman he'd met… I told him that my brother was probably off hiking or camping. I told him not to worry."

"You had no way of knowing. Lucas, it's not your fault. Melanie had plans to go to New York, but they were canceled suddenly. She didn't tell her friends the reason why."

"You think that she was the woman going with Leon?"

"I would assume so," Charlie responded.

"He never told me about her," Lucas said. "I was always

accusing him of being a womanizer. I told Leon I didn't want to meet any of the women he was messing around with. My brother and I used to share an apartment. One night some girlfriend of his vandalized both our cars and tried to break into the place. That's when Valerie and I moved in together. Her ex-roommate was also off-the-wall."

"In view of all this, we will be reopening your brother's investigation as well."

"That's good news. My family will be glad to hear this."

"Lucas, if you can tell me anything else, I'd appreciate you giving me or Detective Leigh a call."

"I will."

As soon as she hung up, the phone on her desk rang again.

"Detective Tesarkee speaking."

"There's someone here to see you," the voice on the other end said. "Sam Tesarkee."

"I'll be right there."

Charlie got up and walked briskly toward the elevator.

What is my father doing here?

Charlie rode the elevator down to the lobby, unable to shake off the feeling of unease. She didn't appreciate her father showing up just like this. Despite their many years of estrangement, Charlie felt a small spark of curiosity. *What does he want?*

When the elevator doors opened, Charlie saw her father sitting in one of the lobby chairs. He stood up.

"What are you doing here?" she asked.

"I saw my doctor earlier today and he confirmed what I already suspected," Sam said. "I have liver cancer. Stage four."

Charlie didn't know how to respond to the information she'd just been given. She wasn't so hard-hearted that she didn't care, but it made her uneasy. It was the same medical condition that killed her mother. "I'm sorry," she managed.

"Charlotte, I've made my peace with God. I would like the chance to make my peace with you."

"Sam, I don't know what to say."

"I just want to sit down and talk. Can we do that?"

"Sure," Charlie responded. "I'm leaving here in an hour. We can go to my place. Have you eaten?"

"Not since breakfast."

"I'll make us some dinner."

"You don't have to go through all that trouble. I don't want to be a bother."

"You won't be," she said. "I'm cooking because I'm hungry."

Sam grinned. "Okay then."

"Just sit here and wait for me."

He nodded. "I'll be right over there in the back."

Charlie ran into Jen at the elevator.

"I'm so proud of you."

"Why?" she asked.

"You didn't have your father thrown out. How is he doing?"

"He's really sick, Jen. Sam has stage four liver cancer."

"Pray for your father, Charlie. Pray for healing."

She groaned and shook her head at the suggestion. "That man never cared anything about me. All he ever wanted was his drink, and my mother was just as bad. He won't get well, I know it. He only wants me in his life now because he's trying to appease God before it's too late."

"I understand why you don't believe, but maybe God can do more than we think if you give Him a chance. I believe that He can heal your heart if you let Him."

"Jen, you know you always walk around here preaching forgiveness. Have you finally forgiven your ex-husband for leaving you?"

"That was a hard one for me," she responded. "I lost my

house because he'd stopped paying the mortgage, and my car was repossessed. My son and I didn't have any place to go. But Grayson saw us one night sitting at a bus stop. He took us to his church and they helped us. One of the members gave us a car and another allowed us to rent an apartment over their garage until we could get back on our feet. Yes, I've forgiven him because had he not been such a horrible person—my life wouldn't have changed for the better."

"You never told me any of that."

"Charlie, I was embarrassed. Grayson—as arrogant as he was, he was truly a blessing to me."

"I'm glad he was there for you. I'm sorry I wasn't."

"I don't hold it against you, Charlie. You couldn't give what you didn't have the capacity to give. Back then you were so angry with the world. You had to work on yourself first." Jen broke into a smile. "And I have to tell you that you've done an amazing job. You're coming out of that shell and letting others see just what a wonderful person you are."

"You've always seen more in me than I see in myself."

"That's because we're our own worst critics."

"Thanks for being my friend," Charlie said just as the doors to the elevator opened.

"You are an amazing cook," Sam exclaimed. He'd been savoring each bite. "I have never tasted a meal like this in my life."

"When I aged out of foster care, it was like going from a lifeboat to a sinking vessel. There wasn't anyone to help me survive, and I had no choice but to learn how to swim."

An audible gasp escaped Sam's mouth as the realization of what he had done hit him. "Charlotte, I can't even begin to explain how much I regret it. Your mother and I were broken when we met—alcohol consumed our lives completely. They now call it trauma bonding. When we had you—we didn't know anything about parenting. Your mother stopped drinking while she was pregnant. She didn't want to hurt you. She wanted to quit for good, but I didn't want to drink alone."

Charlie nodded as she listened.

"I can't undo all that happened. All I know is that I hurt the most precious thing in my life. You were pure and innocent. My mother wanted to raise you, but I refused. She even sat me down with the elders, but I didn't want you raised to be Native. I had turned my back on my heritage. But now, as I sit here and look at you, I see the beauty of our culture in your eyes. I see the resilience and strength of our people in the way you carry yourself."

Tears streamed down Sam's face as he spoke, and Charlie felt her own emotions welling up inside her. She had spent so many years feeling angry and resentful toward her father, but seeing him like this, so vulnerable and remorseful, she couldn't help but feel a twinge of sympathy.

"I want to make it up to you, Charlotte. I want to be the father you deserve."

Charlie sat in silence, taking in her father's words. She had always known that her parents had struggled with alcoholism, but hearing the full extent of it was a shock. She had grown up feeling neglected and abandoned. As she looked at her father, she saw the pain and regret etched on his face.

"I don't know if I can forgive you, Sam," she said after a moment. "But I want to try."

"That is all I ask of you."

Sam insisted on helping her clean the dishes.

When they finished, she said, "You're welcome to spend the night. I can take you back to the Lincoln House on my way to the precinct."

"Are you sure?" he asked.

"I'm a 'say what I mean and mean what I say' kind of girl."

Sam broke into a chuckle. "You got that from your mother."

"Did she love me?" Charlie asked.

"She loved you the best she could, Charlotte. We both did. When you were taken away from us, I thought she would shrivel up and die. She never quite recovered from losing you."

"All you had to do was get better."

"We tried, Charlotte. We both went to rehab. It was court ordered, but the judge still declared that we were unfit to bring you home. By then your mother had been diagnosed with cancer. When she died, I just gave up. I saw you with your foster family once. They had taken you and the other children to the park. The kids were all playing but not you. You sat alone under a tree. My heart broke because I knew we'd done that to you." Tears welled in his eyes once more.

Charlie reached out to him. "Don't, Sam…we have this moment. We have this chance and we're not going to waste it."

Sam smiled through his tears and pulled her into a tight hug.

She didn't want to let her father go, knowing that this moment might be the only one they had together.

When she finally released him, Sam wiped away her tears. "You're all grown up now, Charlotte. You've become such a beautiful woman."

Charlie blushed at his compliment, feeling a sense of pride that she had turned out okay despite all she had been through. "Thanks, Sam. I've had my struggles, but I'm doing alright."

Then they sat up into the early morning talking about her life and all she'd accomplished.

SEVENTEEN

Grayson was on his second cup of coffee when Charlie walked through the doors of the CCU.

She gave him a huge smile. "Good morning."

"Good morning to you, too," he responded. Grayson had never seen her look so happy in all the years he'd known her. "I saw you walking out yesterday with your father."

"We had dinner and he stayed at the house. Sam and I talked until almost one in the morning. It was a good conversation."

He smiled. "I'm so glad to hear that. I've been praying over your situation with your father."

"Can you add a few prayers for me to have more time with my father?" Charlie asked. "He has stage four liver cancer. Grayson, I'm not ready to lose him."

"I will certainly keep him lifted in prayer."

"Thank you," she murmured. "Were you able to find out anything on those calls?"

"Yes," he responded. "I guess Melanie wasn't ready to give him her personal phone number so that's why she used the IP one. I saw your note about the trip to New York and I agree with you—she was his plus-one. Leon had purchased four plane tickets on his credit card—one was for her."

"We are going to have to charge Joel officially or let him go," Charlie stated.

Grayson nodded. "I know."

"I guess we have to consider the possibility that he isn't our killer. I haven't been able to find anything to connect the Armstrongs to Leon. Melanie was so secretive about their budding relationship—there's no way Joel would have known anything about it."

"Unless he was having her followed," Grayson suggested. "He certainly had the money to hire a private detective."

Charlie sank down in her chair. "We need something solid to lead us in the right direction."

Grayson raised his eyes heavenward. *We'd really appreciate Your help.*

Charlie and Grayson had just walked out of their meeting with Phillipa when he received a phone call.

After a short conversation, he hung up saying, "Lucas is in the hospital. He was stabbed."

Her mouth dropped open in surprise. "What? Where?"

"He's here in Charlotte."

She sent a text to Phillipa as they left the building.

When they arrived at the hospital, they were met by his girlfriend Sybil.

"What happened?" Charlie asked.

"I don't know. I came home and found him bleeding on the floor," she responded. "He had a knife in his hand. I gave it to the officer when he arrived."

"Did he try to kill himself?" Grayson asked.

Sybil shook her head no. "Someone attacked him. He told me he was coming to town to spend some time with me before he had to fly out. He also said he wanted to check in with you because he thinks he might know who killed Leon."

"Did he tell you anything else?"

"No, just said he wanted to talk to you. He did say it had something to do with the knife that was used to kill his brother. When Leon died, Lucas gave me a set of custom knives that belonged to his brother. I'm a chef and he thought I'd appreciate them. They're great."

"That's what you gave to the officer?" Grayson asked.

"Yes."

Charlie inquired, "Were there any missing from the set?"

"No, they're all there. There wasn't any type of logo or markings of any kind to indicate the bladesmith," Sybil said. "The craftsmanship is excellent. I'm surprised the person who made them didn't want to brand them. I asked Lucas if he knew who'd made them and all he said was that it was a gift from some woman. He said Leon had a lot of girlfriends and he didn't know which one had given it to him."

"He must have found out," Grayson said.

"Whoever it was called and asked for them back. That's why he decided to come to Charlotte. I'd never seen him so upset. I told him that she could have them. I tried to get him to talk to me, to tell me what was going on, but Lucas kept saying that he didn't want me involved. He said I'd find out soon enough."

"I'm going to speak with the officer about the knife in evidence," Charlie stated. "Grayson, you stay with Sybil. I'll let you know if anything comes of it."

She found the officer and spoke with him. He showed her the photograph of the weapon.

Charlie eyed the photograph. She was disappointed to find that it wasn't the knife used in Melanie's or Leon's murders, although there were some similarities.

On her way back to the floor where she'd left Grayson, Charlie received a phone call bearing good news. A wine expert she'd reached out to just told her that the Italian bottle of wine was sold in only one place in Charlotte. During the initial investigation, Melanie's uncle had told her that it was only sold in Italy.

Charlie rode the elevator to the fourth floor.

When she got off, she found Sybil speaking with a nurse.

"Everything okay?"

"The doctors are doing everything possible to save Lucas," Grayson said. "It's touch-and-go."

Charlie shook her head sadly. "We've got to find this person, and soon."

"Phillipa decided to release Brittany."

"It was probably the right thing to do," she responded as she sat down in one of the visitor chairs.

Grayson sat down beside her. "Find out anything on the knife?"

"I believe they're all made by the same person," Charlie said. "They don't have a logo or signature, but there's something very similar about them. The material is the same. The person who made them—I'd bet it's either a side gig or a hobby. They seem to keep it low-key—maybe to remain a cash-only business."

"So do you think they would advertise?" Grayson asked.

"No. I think they only make them for family or close friends—someone special."

"Like a boyfriend."

"Yes. Lucas told us that Leon was a womanizer," Charlie responded. "Maybe one of his women found out about him and Melanie. She made a huge mistake when she called Lucas and asked him to return them after all these years."

"He must have recognized her and that's why she tried to kill him."

She agreed. "Oh, and I found out where the bottle of wine

came from. There's only one place here in Charlotte that sells it. Bella's Wine Bar."

"I'll stay here at the hospital with Lucas while you check it out," Grayson suggested.

Charlie stood up. "Keep me posted on his condition."

She called the bar and spoke with the owner before heading there. They were close to finding the killer. Charlie could feel it.

Charlie parked in the lot of Bella's Wine Bar. According to the reviews, Bella's was known for its gourmet cheese platters and high-end wines.

The owner, Sergio Bellagambo, greeted her with a warm smile. "Come in, Detective."

"Thank you for seeing me." Charlie showed him a photograph of Melanie Goins. "I know it's been a long time, but do you remember if she ever came into your establishment?"

"Of course I remember her. She was murdered…the poor thing. Her face was all over the news. That's not why I remember her though. She used to come here with a friend." He paused a moment, then said, "We checked IDs. I didn't know she was…"

"I understand. I'm aware of her fake ID card."

Sergio's face softened as he recalled the night he introduced the new brand of wine to his customers, six weeks before Melanie's death. "The wine is from my family's vineyards in Cortona, Province of Arezzo, Italy."

"That explains why you're the only place it can be purchased locally."

"Yes."

He pulled out an old photo album from behind the bar and flipped through the pages, searching for a picture of the evening. "These were taken that night. The night I debuted the wine."

As they examined each image, Melanie immediately stood out with her bright green dress, but Charlie didn't see any trace of anyone familiar. "Did she come with a date?"

"She was with another woman. They both looked beautiful. But I don't seem to have a photograph of her. Some people are shy when it comes to cameras."

Sergio sighed and closed the album; there was no evidence of the woman who had been with Melanie that fateful night.

EIGHTEEN

Grayson could read the frustration on Charlie's face.

"Hey, why don't you go spend some time with your father," he suggested. "Take a mental break from this case."

"I feel like we get so close and then we hit a brick wall."

"As soon as Lucas wakes up, we'll know the identity of the person who tried to kill him and who murdered his brother and Melanie. We will get the answers we need. Now go spend time with your dad."

"I'm only a phone call away."

He smiled. "Goodbye, Charlie."

"Thank you."

Grayson gave a slight nod.

Charlie walked down the cold, empty hallway. The fluorescent lights flickered overhead, casting shadows on the walls. As she walked, her mind drifted back to the case.

Every lead they had turned up had led to a dead end. Melanie and Leon had been brutally murdered, and they still had no idea who was behind it. Charlie felt like she was failing. She had promised Phillipa and the Goins family that they would find the killer, no matter what it took.

She wasn't at the point of giving up, but she really wanted this win. Not for herself or the police department. Charlie wanted it for Melanie's family.

She considered talking things through with Grayson, but something stopped her. Maybe it was the exhaustion that came from weeks of working around the clock. Maybe it was the fear that they might never catch the killer. Or maybe it was the sudden realization that she just wanted to hear his voice.

Charlie took a deep breath and turned off her phone. She was anxious about the short drive to Lincoln House, and what might await her there. Sam Tesarkee was sitting on the porch as she arrived, reading so intently from his Bible that he hadn't noticed her car pull up. With a mix of curiosity and unease, Charlie quietly watched him a moment before getting out of the car. A smile lit up his face when he saw Charlie. "Aren't you supposed to be working?"

"I was and then I realized that I needed a break, so I came to see if you'd be interested in having lunch with me."

"Nothing would make me happier," he responded.

Charlie took a seat next to Sam on the porch swing, feeling the warmth of the sun on her face. They sat in silence for a few moments, until Sam finally spoke.

"I've been praying for you, Charlotte," he said. "I know these past years have been difficult for you, but I believe that God has a plan for your life."

Charlie felt a lump form in her throat as she listened to Sam's words. She just wasn't sure if she still believed. But there was something about the way Sam spoke that made her feel comforted. "Thanks, Sam," she said quietly. "I appreciate your prayers."

They sat in silence again, the only sound being the creaking of the swing as they moved back and forth. Charlie couldn't help but think about how different her life would have been if her parents had made other choices. If they'd chosen her over the alcohol. But they couldn't undo the past.

However, they had the opportunity to change the narrative going forward. She and Sam could do things differently.

Charlie had hesitated for a moment, unsure of what to say to her father. But as they sat on the swing, she could see the sincerity in his eyes. It was clear that he had changed, that he wanted to make amends for his past mistakes. All Charlie had to do was take a leap of faith. Give her father another chance.

She took in the frayed edges of his clothes—worn and faded from frequent use, the holes in the fabric just barely visible. Sam's shoes had seen better days, covered in dust and dirt. "Before we eat though, we're getting you a haircut and going shopping," she announced. "I want to buy you some shoes and whatever else you need."

"Charlotte..."

"This isn't charity, Sam. I'm doing it because I want to buy my dad some nice clothes. You deserve it."

Sam grinned from ear to ear, his eyes sparkling with gratitude. "Thank you, Charlotte."

He closed his Bible and stood up, wincing a little as he stretched his legs. "Let's go then—I could use some new shoes."

Charlie followed Sam down the porch steps and out to her car, the sleek gray SUV gleaming in the midday sun. The drive to the mall was short, and soon they were walking through the bustling corridors, passing by glittering storefronts and excited shoppers.

She led Sam to a high-end shoe store, where a saleswoman with a professional smile greeted them. "Good afternoon, how can I help you?"

Charlie turned to Sam. "Pick out any pair of shoes you want, Sam. Anything at all."

Sam hesitated, looking around nervously. "I don't want to impose, Charlotte. These shoes are too expensive."

"Nonsense," Charlie said. "Everybody needs at least one good pair of shoes."

After Sam found the perfect pair for him, Charlie made the purchase and took him to a clothing store.

"These shoes feel like heaven," he told her. "I never knew shoes could feel this comfortable. Thank you, Charlotte."

She took his hand in hers. "I was happy to do it, Sam."

Charlie purchased several outfits for him before leaving to get his hair cut.

Once that was done, Sam said, "I feel like a new man."

She chuckled. "You look like a new man, too."

"Let me pay you back for some of this stuff, Charlotte. I get a disability check."

She shook her head. "Please let me be your daughter for the time we have left. I was never able to help you before. Let me do it now. Sam, it's hard to explain but it brings me so much joy to be able to be here for you. You're not alone anymore."

He hugged her. "Let me be your father then. And as your father, I'd like to buy my beautiful daughter lunch."

Blinking back happy tears, Charlie nodded. "Okay."

When she returned to the hospital later that evening, Grayson took one look at her and smiled. "I take it lunch went well."

"I just had a wonderful time with my dad. Thank you for suggesting it. You were right. I needed to take a break from the case." Charlie glanced around. "Where is Sybil?"

"She went home to get some sleep. She'll be back later."

"How is Lucas doing?"

"He's holding his own," Grayson responded. "The doctors are more optimistic about him pulling through."

"That's great news," Charlie said. "Have you been able to see him?"

He shook his head. "He hasn't woken up yet. I plan on staying here until he does."

"I hadn't expected you to do anything else."

"Is it my imagination or are you warming up to me?" Grayson asked with a grin.

Charlie rolled her eyes, but couldn't hide the small smile that tugged at the corners of her lips. "Don't flatter yourself, Grayson. I'm just saying that I know how much you really care about people. It's great that Lucas has someone like you looking out for him."

His grin grew wider, and his eyes twinkled mischievously. "Oh, come on, Charlie. We both know there's more to it than that."

Charlie raised an eyebrow at him. "Is there?"

"You can deny it all you want," he said. "But I can tell that you feel something for me."

She scoffed. "And what gave you that idea?"

"The way you look at me," Grayson said confidently. He didn't want to play games with her. It was time Charlie knew he had feelings for her. And that he knew she felt something for him as well.

Charlie looked away as if feeling embarrassed.

Grayson chuckled, closing the distance between them. "I'm not going to pressure you into anything, Charlie. But just know that I feel the same way about you. And if and when you're ready—we can talk."

Her phone vibrated.

Charlie looked at it. "Sergio just sent me a text. A photo actually. He says it had fallen out of the photo album he showed me the other night and he just found it and send a copy to me."

Stunned, she showed it to Grayson.

"I'm going to pay her a visit."

"I should be there with you."

"I'm fine. You stay here and wait for Lucas to wake up. I'm just going over there to get some clarification on why Tabitha never mentioned this. Like everything else, it's probably another dead end."

Charlie was grateful for Sergio's timing. It couldn't have been any better. She had suspected that Grayson had feelings for her, then Jen had all but confirmed it, but until now he had never said a word.

But as much as she wanted to be excited about the possibility of starting something with him, she couldn't help but feel worried, too. They worked together; knowing that their relationship could potentially bring career risks weighed heavily on her mind. If things didn't work out between them, would it make going to work every day unbearable?

Charlie mulled over the situation as she walked toward the elevator. She called Jen while she waited.

"You know, Charlie, sometimes you just have to take a leap of faith," Jen said after hearing what happened between her and Grayson.

Charlie was grateful for Jen's support. She had always been a good friend to her and she trusted her.

"I know," she said. "It's just that I don't want to make the wrong decision. I don't want to mess up my career or our partnership."

"I understand. But sometimes, you have to take a risk to get what you want. And if Grayson is what you want, then you should go for it. Look at how things worked out between Phillipa and Kyle."

"They had history, Jen."

"True, but you've known Grayson for a long time."

"You're right. Even when I couldn't stand him—it was more of a me issue. He hadn't ever done anything to me."

The elevator doors opened, and she stepped inside.

"I'll call you later. I'm in the elevator."

Charlie leaned against the wall, lost in thought. Jen was right. She had been playing it safe for too long. Maybe it was time to take a chance on love. But before she could focus on herself—she had to find Melanie's killer.

NINETEEN

Charlie sat in her car long enough to make a phone call to Kathy.

"Why don't you leave me alone?"

"I'm just trying to do my job," she responded. "The only reason I'm calling you is to ask if Melanie and Tabitha often spent time together."

"Not really," Kathy said. "I mean they attended some wine tastings together, but that's about it. They seemed to bond over wine but didn't have anything else in common. I'm sure Tabitha would have told you about that. Why do you ask?"

"We're checking every single piece of information we discover."

"Can you tell me why Joel's still in jail?"

"No, it's not something we're ready to discuss with the public," Charlie said. "Thanks, Kathy."

She hung up and got out of the vehicle.

Tabitha opened the door and greeted Charlie with a warm smile. Welcoming her in, she stepped aside. "Detective Tesarkee…what brings you here to my door again?"

"I see you're still recovering," Charlie said, gesturing to the brace on her foot.

"It isn't healing as quickly as the doctor initially thought so he's having me wear this a little longer."

They sat down in the living room, Tabitha on the sofa and Charlie in an accent chair closest to the door.

"I'm just following up on some new leads. I was wondering if there is anything about Melanie that you didn't tell me?"

Tabitha shook her head. "I'm sorry—I don't have anything new to share. It was a quiet night for the most part until I heard the noises. I've already told you all that. I appreciate that you're so dedicated to finding Melanie's killer. You just don't seem to give up."

Looking her straight in the eye, Charlie responded, "I want justice for my victims."

"I admire your fortitude."

Charlie noted the glass of wine and the charcuterie tray on the coffee table. Pointing, she said, "You're a wine drinker." She wondered if Tabitha was still on pain medication.

Tabitha gave her a look of confusion. "Yes, I enjoy wine. It relaxes me. Would you like a glass?"

She shook her head no. "I don't drink. Did you know that Melanie also liked wine? In fact, she had quite a collection in her apartment. She has an uncle who also collects wine. I'm sure she must have mentioned it to you."

"Why would you say that?"

Charlie decided to be straightforward. "Tabitha, I know that you and Melanie went to Bella's Wine Bar six weeks before she died. I'm a bit confused as to why you never mentioned this in your statement. You led me to believe that you were nothing more than neighbors."

"We went to one wine bar. That doesn't make us friends."

"I suppose you're right, but I spoke with Kathy before I got out of the car. I found out that it wasn't just once. This was something you and Melanie did quite often."

"I got busy," Tabitha said tersely. "Detective, I've cooperated with you from the very beginning, but I don't like where this is heading. You're looking in the wrong direction."

Charlie eyed her, looking for any sign of deception.

Suddenly, Tabitha's eyes widened and she looked at her with a newfound urgency. "Wait, I just remembered something. I didn't think it was important before, but now I think it might be. Melanie used to date a football player. Joel Armstrong. I heard her talking to him on the phone a few days before she was killed. They were arguing about something. I couldn't hear exactly what, but it sounded tense. I know that he and his wife were in custody. You let the wife go but kept him. I'm really sorry I didn't remember until now."

"He's been cleared of any wrongdoing." She was lying to gauge Tabitha's reaction.

"I see…well, I've told you everything I know."

Meeting her gaze, Charlie said, "I can see it in your face, Tabitha. There's more you want to say."

Tabitha's eyes narrowed, and her gaze shifted between Charlie and her own hands. "I really don't like to speak ill of the dead, but you're giving me no choice, Detective. The truth is that Melanie wasn't as innocent as she looked. She was promiscuous and she didn't care about who she hurt. She thought she was better than Kat. I never liked the way she treated her. When we'd go out, I'd try to speak to her about it. I wanted to help her see the error of her ways before it was too late." She changed her position in her chair and leaned forward, picking up a piece of cheese from the plate in front of her and biting off a small chunk before setting it back down and chewing slowly.

"Too late for what?"

Charlie's gaze returned to the knife on the charcuterie tray that Tabitha had just used. The handle was similar to the custom set of knives that was given to Leon. She drew her gaze back to Tabitha. "Explain what you meant by saying that."

"Just that she could end up in some trouble. Like messing with that married football player. Didn't you talk to his wife? Maybe she's the person who killed Melanie. Y'all had her down at the jail, too. Melanie got mixed up with the wrong folk—that's what happened."

Tabitha leaned forward in her chair, her face crumpling with emotion. Her eyes cast down, her mouth set in a line, as if she was struggling to find the right words. "She wasn't the person you thought she was."

Noting her body language and her tone, Charlie said, "Tabitha, you seem angry. Did Melanie do something to you?"

"Disappointed is more like it. I extended my friendship to that woman. The night we went to that wine bar, I was meeting up with the man I'd been seeing. I introduced Melanie to him—he basically ignored me and began flirting with Melanie all night. I finally got fed up and I left."

"Are you saying that she was receptive to his flirting?" Charlie asked.

"Of course she was. Women like her love attention."

"You left her there with your boyfriend?"

"It was like I was invisible," Tabitha uttered. "I wasn't about to hang around like the third wheel."

"Why did you invite her to attend an event if you were meeting your date there?"

"Melanie heard about it and begged to come with me. Trust me… I never intended to tell her about it in the first place. I think somewhere deep inside me, I knew what was going to happen."

"What was his name?" Charlie asked.

Tabitha continued as if she never heard the question.

"He made me so happy. He made me feel beautiful. I developed alopecia as a child—I was forced to wear wigs, which resulted in a lot of cruel teasing and bullying by the popular girls. I've never met a man so handsome who wanted *me*."

Charlie nodded with understanding. "So, *Leon* made you feel good about yourself."

Tabitha smiled wistfully. "Yes, he did. He had a way of making me forget all my problems and insecurities. We had something special."

"What happened between him and Melanie?" Charlie pressed.

Tabitha sighed as if the memory was still fresh in her mind. "I went to the bathroom and when I came back, they were kissing. I couldn't believe it. I left them there."

Charlie shook her head in disbelief. "Did you ever try to reach out to Leon after that?"

Tabitha shook her head. "No. I was too hurt and humiliated. I didn't want to give him the satisfaction of knowing how much it hurt me."

"What about later? Did you ever confront them?"

Tabitha's expression changed.

"That's when I knew I had to pay them back. I was tired of being used and mistreated. I decided not to let it happen again. I was going to take back my power. I sent her a note that said I wasn't stupid. Melanie had told me about the one she left for Kat when she found out about the affair with Joel. She came to my apartment, handed it to me and laughed."

"Is that when you decided to kill them?"

Tabitha took a deep breath, her eyes fixed on Charlie. "Yes," she finally said, "that's exactly what I did, Detective."

Charlie leaned forward in her chair. "You killed both of them?"

Tabitha nodded, her voice barely above a whisper. "I convinced Leon to meet me on the bike trail he loved so much. I told him how he made me feel and that I understood that it was all Melanie's fault. She was a seductress. That's when he told me that it was over between us. He said he wanted Melanie and had invited her to go to New York with him. I stabbed him where his heart should have been."

Her face turned cold and she broke into a wild laugh. "She was already packing her bags for her upcoming trip. You should've seen her face when she found out Leon was dead. I took great pleasure in telling her that someone had killed him."

Charlie watched as Tabitha's hands curled into fists, her breathing coming out in harsh gasps. The room felt suffocating, as if the air had grown thick with the weight of the woman's anger.

"She had no idea I'd done it until that night I walked into her apartment."

"Tabitha, how did you know that the door was unlocked?" Charlie asked.

"Kat didn't know I was sitting outside on my patio while she was talking to that football player. Did you know that she was sleeping with him, too? They had some drama going on up in that apartment. That night Joel showed up and his wife, too. When they left, I paid Melanie a visit."

Charlie swallowed hard, then asked, "What happened between you two that night?"

"I told her that I'd killed Leon. That I'd come to make her pay.

"We got into a fight, but I was able to overpower her. I pulled out my knife..."

Grayson wanted to shout when Sybil rushed out of the hospital room saying that Lucas had finally opened his eyes. He sent up a quick prayer of thanksgiving.

"I'm glad to see you," he said when he entered the room.

"I'm glad you're seeing me in this hospital bed and not in the morgue." Leon tried to move, the effort causing him to grimace.

"Just relax," Grayson stated. "You have to let your body heal from the trauma."

"It was Tabitha Raines who killed my brother and Melanie. I figured it out when she called me and asked for the knives. She told me that she'd made them special for Leon. She came to my girl's apartment and I confronted her. I told her that she wouldn't get away with it. She stabbed me and that's all I remember."

"Charlie's with her now," Grayson said. "I need to leave, but I'll be back."

"Go," Lucas responded. "That woman is unstable. I didn't know Leon was messing with her—I could've told him she wasn't right."

Grayson rushed out of the hospital room and quickly grabbed an elevator. He had to get to Charlie and make sure that she was safe.

He knew she was capable of handling herself, but Charlie wasn't just his partner. She was the woman he loved.

As he reached the ground floor, Grayson's heart was racing. He didn't know what he would do if something happened to her.

He made his way through the crowds, dodging doctors and nurses as they rushed about.

Grayson hurried though the parking deck and located his car.

He'd already alerted Phillipa and was on his way to offer assistance. Grayson tried calling Charlie but it went straight to voice mail, which left him with a bad feeling.

"Call me back," he whispered. "C'mon, call me back, Charlie."

He got in and slammed the door shut, taking a deep breath to calm his racing heart. Grayson started the car and peeled out of the parking garage, not caring about the honking horns and angry shouts that followed behind him.

He had to get to Charlie.

As he drove, Grayson tried calling her once more, but it went straight to voice mail again. He slammed his hand on the steering wheel.

Tabitha didn't live too far from the hospital but it seemed like it was taking too long to get to her place.

Charlie felt her phone vibrating once again. She had an idea that it was Grayson, but she didn't want anything to stop Tabitha from talking. She knew he'd send backup if he didn't come himself.

She just wanted to keep Tabitha calm until she could figure out a way to take control and get them both safely out of the apartment.

"I understand what you went through," Charlie said. "My life wasn't a prize either. I had to deal with bullying, but I found other ways to cope with it."

"Melanie stole the only man who ever loved me. I had to make her pay."

"Tabitha, do you really believe that Leon loved you? He had a reputation of being quite the ladies' man."

"A man is gonna do what he's gonna do. Melanie should have known how to keep her hands off someone else's man. She sure didn't like it when Kat was messing around with Joel."

Charlie wanted to keep her talking while she figured out her next steps.

"I'm sure you wouldn't have liked it if she'd taken your man," Tabitha uttered.

"I guess you and I see things differently," Charlie said. "If some other woman can take my man—he really wasn't mine in the first place."

Tabitha suddenly grabbed a knife that was hidden behind one of the pillows on the sofa and lunged at Charlie.

Charlie leaped out of the way just in time, her heart racing and her mind reeling. She had anticipated danger, but the suddenness of the attack still took her by surprise. Tabitha was clearly consumed by anger and jealousy over a man who likely never cared about her as much as she thought he did.

"Tabitha, put the knife down. Let's talk this out," Charlie said calmly, trying to defuse the tense situation. She didn't want to have to pull her gun and shoot. But Tabitha wasn't listening.

She lunged at Charlie again.

Thinking quickly, Charlie grabbed a nearby lamp and swung it at Tabitha, narrowly missing her head.

The woman stumbled backward, fumbling for the knife, but Charlie was already on her, tackling her to the ground.

They grappled for a few moments, Charlie using her strength and agility to keep Tabitha subdued. The woman growled and hissed like a feral animal, the intense look in her eyes sending chills down Charlie's spine.

Finally, she managed to pin Tabitha's arms behind her back, restraining her.

Tabitha's struggles gradually subsided. Her eyes filled with tears and she sobbed uncontrollably.

TWENTY

Grayson's heart was pounding in his chest as he pulled up to Tabitha's apartment building.

He parked the car and leaped out, his feet pounding on the pavement as he sprinted up the stairs to her unit. He banged on the door with desperate urgency.

No answer but he could hear someone screaming inside.

His duty weapon out, Grayson burst into Tabitha's apartment and found Charlie on top of the suspect. He was relieved to see his partner alive and in control.

"You okay?" he asked.

Breathing hard, she nodded.

Beneath her, Tabitha's eyes were wild as her screams echoed off the walls as complete panic seemed to take hold of her.

Grayson rushed forward to help Charlie restrain the suspect. He grabbed hold of her flailing arms and pressed them down to the ground.

Tabitha continued to scream and thrash around, making it difficult for them to hold her down.

"Calm down, Tabitha," Grayson said. "We're going to get you some help. No one wants to harm you. We just don't want you to hurt yourself."

But his words fell unnoticed as Tabitha continued to scream

and struggle. It was clear that she was in the grips of some kind of breakdown.

Charlie looked at Grayson with concern etched on her face. "We need to get her to a hospital."

He nodded in agreement.

Getting Tabitha out of the apartment without causing her harm might be a challenge, but they had to act quickly before the situation got any worse. The apartment was suddenly filled with uniformed officers.

"Okay, Charlie, I'm going to lift her up. You get behind her and help me carry her out," Grayson instructed.

Together, they lifted Tabitha off the ground and started to make their way toward the door. Tabitha's weight made it difficult for them to move quickly and they had to dodge her flailing limbs.

As they made their way down the hallway, they could hear the sounds of shouting and crying coming from the other apartments. Clearly, Tabitha's outburst had caused quite a commotion.

When they finally made it outside, they were faced with a group of concerned neighbors who had gathered. They looked at Grayson and Charlie with alarm, clearly worried about Tabitha's condition.

"Is she okay?" one of them asked.

Grayson nodded, trying to keep the situation under control. "We're taking her to the hospital. We just need to get her out of here."

With the help of the other officers, they managed to get Tabitha into the back of a police cruiser.

Charlie's eyes flickered and she looked up at him. "Grayson, is Lucas okay?"

"He's stable," he responded. "He woke up and told me about Tabitha. She's the person who made those knives."

"We need to get CSI in there. We might find the murder weapons—at least I hope we will, but even if we don't... I have her full confession."

"I'm not sure she'll be in any condition to stand trial," Grayson said. "But you did it, Charlie. You solved not only the Goins cold case but also Leon Shelby's murder."

Charlie took a deep breath. It was over. But she hadn't done it alone.

"I couldn't have done this without you, Grayson." She looked around at the scene and paused for a moment to take it all in. The flashing red-and-blue lights of the police cruisers, the sound of footsteps rushing about, the wailing of sirens in the distance.

Her nerves were still on edge, but she knew she had to stay focused. She couldn't let her guard down yet. Too much was at stake. "I want to go to the hospital to make sure Tabitha is stabilized and handcuffed to her bed. We can't take any chances. She's not only a danger to others—she's also a danger to herself."

Grayson nodded. "The ambulance should be here shortly."

He waited with her as they watched paramedics load Tabitha into the back of the ambulance.

After speaking with the CSI team, they left and headed to the hospital.

"You're quiet over there," he said.

"I was thinking about Melanie," Charlie responded. "She didn't deserve to die before her time. I also feel bad for Tabitha. She let her bitterness take root and... I realized that I'd done the same thing. Let bitterness consume my life."

"She never moved past her pain, but you found a way to do so, Charlie. I feel sorry for Tabitha and I'll pray for her."

"She's probably going to be locked up for the rest of her life."

Grayson nodded. “She will either be in prison or a psychiatric hospital. Either way, it’s for the best.”

“I know. I was thinking about the first time I met her. Tabitha seemed so nice and sweet. I had no idea that she’d murdered not one person but two.” Charlie looked out the window. “I spoke with Kathy and she confirmed that Tabitha and Melanie attended wine tastings regularly. She thought I already knew about it since I’d interviewed Tabitha. I’d missed that little tidbit.”

“It’s easy to do,” Grayson said. “I’m sure you asked her about her relationship with Melanie.”

“I did,” Charlie confirmed. “And she lied. They all lied to me.”

“It happens all the time.”

“I know. I just never had a case where everyone lies—everybody seemed to have a secret.”

He glanced over at her and grinned. “I hate to tell you this but it won’t be your last, I’m afraid.”

“Great,” Charlie uttered.

At the hospital, she told Grayson, “My dad had an appointment at the cancer center. I’m going to check on him. I’ll meet up with you in a few minutes.”

He took her by the hand. “Let him know that I’m praying for him.”

“Thank you. I’ll tell him.”

Grayson surprised them both when he stepped close to her, reaching out to cup Charlie’s face in his hand.

For a second, her body went still before she tilted her face up toward him, at the same time that he leaned down to her. The kiss was quick, but perfect.

She pulled away. “I didn’t see that coming,” she said, her voice shaking slightly.

“Me neither,” he said. “It just felt right.”

Grayson’s heart was racing in his chest. The thought of

something happening to Charlie when she was alone with Tabitha—he had promised himself that he was going to let her know exactly how he felt. "You have no idea how much I care about you."

Charlie put a hand to his lips. "Hold that thought until later tonight. Let's close this case officially, then we can finish this conversation."

He nodded.

Charlie turned and hurried off toward the cancer center.

Charlie released a sigh of relief when she saw her father.

He took one look at her and said, "Something happened."

"I just solved the Goins murder."

He hugged her. "Congratulations. Why don't you look happy?"

"It's a sad situation, Dad. There are no winners here. A woman is being hospitalized in the psychiatric hospital and I'm not sure she'll ever recover. She killed two people and almost murdered someone else."

"You did your job, Charlotte. This woman will hopefully get the help she needs."

Charlie nodded. "I hope so. I came to check on you. Have you had your treatment yet?"

"I'm waiting for them to call me back there," Sam said.

"I'll wait with you."

"Are you aware that you called me Dad?"

"Yes, because right now I need my dad."

"I'm here, sweetheart."

Sam's eyes softened as he pulled Charlie in closer to him.

She was all grown up now, a successful detective with a tough exterior, but Charlie knew that her father could see the vulnerability in her eyes. She felt just like a little girl, clinging for safety when she was scared or hurt. Only now, her father was here to comfort her. And she had Grayson, too.

They sat in silence for a few moments, waiting for the nurse to call Sam back for his treatment. Charlie's mind drifted back to the case she had just solved. It was one of the toughest cases she had worked on in her career as a detective. The Goins murder had shaken the entire town.

She knew that CSI was still at the apartment searching every inch of Tabitha's home until their white-gloved hands found any evidence that might link her to the murders of Leon and Melanie.

For the time being, she enjoyed sitting here with her father and being his daughter.

"Tabitha had kept the knives she used to murder both Leon and Melanie," Grayson said, hanging up the phone the next morning. "The lab tried calling you, but you were in your meeting with Phillipa."

"I saw that they called," Charlie responded. "I'm glad they reached out to you. We have our proof. The only question I have is why she wanted the knives back that she'd given Leon. If she'd kept her mouth shut—we'd probably still be scratching our heads."

He nodded. "She got antsy. That's the only explanation. I believe reopening this case was a trigger for Tabitha."

Charlie nodded. "I can't help feeling that I pushed too hard with Tabitha."

"You didn't push her over the edge, if that's what you're thinking. It was her guilt," Grayson said. "The woman was struggling, Charlie. What happened to her isn't on you."

Charlie took a deep breath and let it out slowly, feeling a weight lift off her chest. But the unease remained. "I know. But I can't shake the feeling that I made things worse. Maybe if I hadn't prompted her to relive what happened..."

Grayson shook his head. "You did what you had to do. And even if you hadn't, there's no telling what might have happened. Tabitha was a ticking time bomb. She needed help and she didn't get it in time. She would've killed someone else."

Charlie nodded. "I just wish we could've done something sooner."

Grayson put a comforting hand on her shoulder. "We did all we could."

Charlie sat down in the empty chair beside his desk. "I told you before that we make a great team and I meant it. Phillipa asked me if I wanted to make it permanent."

"What did you say?"

She smiled. "I told her that I'd think about it."

"I thought we had a good thing going," Grayson said.

"We do and I'd like to keep it separate from work," Charlie responded. "I really like you. More than I ever thought I could. I would rather build from that."

"I hear you."

"Are you okay with not being my partner then?"

Grayson nodded.

"I asked my dad to move in with me," Charlie announced. "He doesn't need to be in the Lincoln House while he's going through his treatments. They make him so weak. I spoke with Jen's cousin who is a retired nurse and she's going to stay with him on the days he has his treatments."

"Sounds like you have it all figured out."

"Do you think I'm rushing things?"

Grayson replied, "Not at all. He's your father and it's normal to want to spend as much time with him as possible. I would've done the same thing."

Charlie was relieved that Grayson had taken her decision so well. She had been holding back her feelings for a long time, afraid of ruining their professional relationship. But now, after everything they had just been through together, a future with Grayson seemed possible. Their eyes met, and in that moment, Charlie knew that she had made the right choice.

EPILOGUE

Charlie stood before the altar in a strapless white wedding dress with a pair of silver rhinestone sandals peeking out from beneath the hem of her dress. In her hand, a simple bouquet of flowers—lilies of the valley and roses—she clung to it as if it were her lifeline. She parted her lips, flashing a smile at Grayson, the man she was going to spend the rest of her life with.

When she glanced over at Sam, Charlie beamed with joy. She was thankful that he was well enough to walk her down the aisle and she looked forward to whatever time they had left together.

The realization that she would never have to face anything alone from then on made this day all the more special for Charlie.

As she and Grayson said their vows, Charlie felt a sense of completeness that she had never felt before. She knew that he was the one for her, and she could not wait to spend the rest of her life with him.

She held on to his hand as they exchanged rings, sealing their love for eternity.

"I love you," he said loud enough for only Charlie to hear.

"I love you, too," she responded.

As the ceremony ended, the newlyweds walked down the

aisle hand in hand. The sun was setting behind them, casting a golden glow over the entire setting.

As they made their way to the reception, Grayson whispered in Charlie's ear, "You look absolutely stunning, sweetheart."

"I'm so happy we're finally married." She had never thought she would be someone's wife. It had never been her dream, but it was now her beautiful reality.

Grayson smiled. "Me, too, Charlie. There's nowhere else I'd rather be than by your side."

* * * * *